Me And My Hittas 3

Me and My Hittas 3

By Tranay Adams

Me and My Hittas 3

ISBN: 978-1-7377789-7-4

Email: dopereadzpresents@gmail.com
Facebook: Tranay Adams
Instagram: Tranay Adams
Cover Artist: Divine

Prologue

"Damn, Puppet, is this you?" Mira asked, rounding a drop-top money green Chevy Malibu with white leather interior. It had an airbrushed image of a sexy Mexican lady wearing a sombrero on its hood. She wore chain-bullets over both her shoulders and held twin smoking revolvers in each hand. The smoke wafting from the pistols spelled out Puppet's neighborhood.

Mira eyed Puppet seductively while licking her top lip. Her long blonde hair flowed over her face, but left just enough space between the strands for her to peer through. The glare she gave her suitor was one of a hungry lioness looking to pounce on its next kill to feed its cubs. Mira was a tan skinned honey with ample breasts and a small waist that protruded to a pair of wide hips and even thicker legs. She didn't have much ass, but her shortcomings were easily forgiven when compared to her other attributes.

Puppet watched Mira from behind the wheel of his finely tuned machine. His almond brown eyes followed her without him having to move his neck. He felt a hard-on coming to life inside of his Ben Davis jeans as she circled his whip in her bleach stained Daisy Duke's. The shorts were cut at the beginning of her thighs and were so high up you could see her ass cheeks peeking out beneath them. Puppet licked his lips and brushed across the thin mustache above his top-lip, imagining himself balls deep in Mira. Seeing the imprint of her hard nipples through her sky blue spaghetti strap shirt gave him a tingly feeling in his loins. Little momma was sex playing him and it was working, because he was just about ready to hop out of his ride and ravage her like a sex starved deviant.

Puppet had been chasing Mira since last summer, but she'd never given him any play. It wasn't until he started hustling for his big brother Creeper, and got his cheddar up that she gave him a double take. Puppet was handling a little change and money was Mira's open sesame.

"Ohhh, is this real gold?" Mira asked, wearing an expression of surprise with her puckered thin lips as she kneeled down to one of the gold Dayton spokes the Malibu was sitting on. She gave her golden reflection the once over as she stared into the wire rim. Her kneeling down revealed more of those luscious thighs of hers and caused Puppet to sit up in his seat, lifting his black sunglasses to the top of his head for a better look of her.

"Yeah, that's real gold, baby," he lied smoothly. "I don't know how the Vatos do it on your side, but we're real playas over here, feel me? Why don't chu stop bullshitting and come take a ride with me, chica? Come do the town up with a young boss." he rested his gold, jeweled hand on the windowsill hoping it would entice her, and it did. Especially once the streetlights bounced off of it and set off an explosion of twinkles. The gold Virgin Mary medallion resting against his long sleeve cocaine white T-shirt helped as well.

"You want me to take a ride with ju, papi?" Mira asked, leaning over into his car, purposely boasting her cleavage. "Where are we going?"

"Where ever you want to, momma," he replied, letting his eyes take her in from head to toe. "It's your world, baby girl."

"Alright, just let me tell my homegirl I'm leaving," she told him and yelled out across the street to her friend's house. "Havana, I'ma 'bout to roll out with Puppet, I'll be back later, aye?"

"Bye, bitch," Havana yelled back. "Make sure homeboy straps up. You don't wanna be getting all pregnant and shit."

"Please, bitch, ain't no body doing nothing," she claimed. "We're just going for a ride, that's all."

"Sure," Havana said. "Lie to daddy, but tell mommy the truth."

"Whatever, puta," Mira gave her the middle-finger as she ran to hop in on the passenger side of Puppet's ride.

Puppet cruised the streets slumped down in his seat with a bad ass bitch on the passenger side. The reflection of the city reflected on the windshield of his Chevy Malibu. He nodded his head to the tunes of The Delfonic's that flowed softly from his speakers. He didn't have a specific destination, but he wanted to be where everyone could see him in his fly ass ride with his sexy chica.

Mira turned the stereo down and asked, "Do you have any coke?"

Puppet nodded and pulled out his ashtray. He fished around inside until he produced a tiny bundle of cocaine. The powdered substance shined and boasted its purity and potency. Seeing this caused Mira's eyes to bug and her mouth to water, she licked her lips. If it was nothing more she loved in the world it was some good cocaine. She tried to snatch the bag from Puppet's fingers and he yanked it back.

"Relax, baby, this ain't for lil' girls," he told her. "this is grown folks business. This is the real deal, nah mean?"

"I snorted coke before, Puppet. Gimmie that," she tried to grab the bundle and he yanked it back again.

"I'm sure you have, but it wasn't nothing like this." Puppet assured her. "This ain't that garbage you be getting from Pickles, that you and your homegirls be shoveling up your noses. That crap been remixed so much that half of it ain't even coke."

"I'ma big girl, Puppet, I can handle it…," she grabbed his hand and sucked his middle-finger. "Among other things," She said sensually, biting down gently on her tongue and staring up at him seductive.

Feeling Mira's hot, wet tongue on his finger brought back that tingly feeling in Puppet's loins and he imagined what her mouth would feel like wrapped around his pole. He smiled as the thought popped up in his head and he tossed the bundle in her lap. Mira grabbed The Delfonic's CD case and dumped the contents of the bag out on it. She diced the cocaine up finely and then separated it into three lines. Taking a rolled up dollar bill, she snorted the first line and then the second. Before she knew it she was feeling the effects of the coke that Puppet warned her about. And he wasn't lying. It was a far more superior product than the stuff she and Havana copped from Pickles boys. Its effects brought her to a utopia she never wanted to leave, not to mention she was feeling horny as hell.

She popped out her tanned breasts and sprinkled the last line across them. She got to her knees in the seat and leaned over to Puppet. Puppet kept one eye on the road as he snorted the cocaine from Mira's breasts. Once all of the cocaine was vacuumed up his nostrils, he licked up the faint traces and sucked on her nipples, drawing soft moans from her lips. He knew he had her going because she had her manicured hand down her Daisy Duke's and was finger fucking herself. He got her to lie back in the seat while his hand took over the job until she came, drenching his soft leather with her juices. Once she'd recovered, she unzipped his jeans and pulled out his brown pole. Using both hands she worked him to an erection and allowed her jaws to engulf him. She made slurping sounds as she glided her mouth back and forth down his meat, spilling her hot saliva down his shaft and balls. She released sensual moans as she took care of her business, which only heightened the experience for Puppet.

Puppet's jaw dropped and his eyes slowly fluttered as if he was trying to stop from falling asleep. Feeling himself about to cum, he groaned and bit his inner jaw. He wanted to bust off, but he also wanted to prolong the experience, which caused him to hold back until he couldn't take it anymore. Puppet grabbed the back of Mira's head and held her down on his dick until he exploded all inside of her mouth, spilling his children down her esophagus. Veins formed in his neck and forehead and he clenched his jaws as he released himself.

"Goddamn, girl, I didn't know you had it like that," Puppet told her as he popped the glove-box open and pulled out a handful of napkins. He tossed a few in her lap and used the others to wipe off his glistening cock.

"You ain't know? You better ask somebody," Mira giggled and smiled as she looked in the sun-visor mirror to wipe her mouth.

"Is that right? Well, I'm tryna find out what that pussy hitting for." He said, balling up the napkin and throwing it out of the window. A police siren went off behind them and startled Puppet. He looked through his rear-view mirror and saw the flashing red and blue lights of an unmarked car. "Oh, shit, the policia." He panicked.

"Ah, damn!" Mira looked back. "You don't have any more coke on you, do you?"

"Nah, but I got my gun under the seat. Fuck," Puppet cursed. "Toss that CD out."

Mira did as she was told. Then she and Puppet tried to make themselves look like they weren't high, which would be hard since the truth was written all over their faces. Puppet pulled to the side of the curb and executed the engine, telling Mira, "Just be cool, alright?" she nodded her understanding.

Puppet turned around as a tall, slender white man approached his door. His eyes narrowed into slits as a bright light was shined in his face from a flashlight. The light swept over to Mira, who also narrowed her eyes. Puppet tried to see the man's face but could only make out a pair of lips surrounded by a five o'clock shadow. The mouth moved like a horse's would when eating hay as the man chewed gum. The man clicked off the flashlight and Puppet was able to see the face the lips belonged to.

"Arsenegger," Puppet frowned. "What the fuck, man? You gotta hard-on for Mexicans or something?"

"Nope, just you, homes." Arsenegger said with a no nonsense attitude. "Now get the fuck outta the car."

"Bullshit, I ain't getting outta nothing." he spat defiantly. "I know my…"

The words died in Puppet's throat as Arsenegger struck him in the head repeatedly with the flashlight. He then opened the door from the inside and pulled him out by the collar of his T-shirt, letting his body hit the street like a dumbbell.

"Do me a favor and step outta the car, sweetheart." Ortiz said holding open the car's passenger-side door. Mira stepped out of the car and was told to place her hands on the trunk of the car with her legs spread. Detective Ortiz checked the car while Detective Arsenegger kept an eye on Puppet and Mira with his gun down at his side.

"Piece of shit, we know it was one of you guys that wasted Sullivan." Arsenegger sneered, speaking of his colleague and good friend that was shot three times at point blank range through the back of the head while he sat behind the wheel of his car waiting for his partner to return with the Chinese takeout they'd ordered. It had been six months and the police didn't have any suspects, but word on the streets was it was someone from Puppet's set.

"Fuck are you talking about, man? I don't know anything about anybody getting killed." Puppet swore, holding the side of his bleeding head.

"You don't know nothing, huh?" Arsenegger mocked his accent. "Somehow I doubt that." He looked around to make sure no one was watching him before stomping and kicking Puppet, causing him to bawl in the street.

"Stop," Mira hollered. "What're you doing? We didn't do anything."

Arsenegger pointed his gun at Mira and said, "Shut your fucking hole, and keep your hands where I can see them."

"Jackpot," Ortiz called out, holding up a Glock .23 by its barrel. The sight of the lethal weapon made Arsenegger smile sinisterly. "Cuff'em, I'll get the girl."

Arsenegger handcuffed Puppet and got him to his feet. He ushered him toward the unmarked car with him talking shit all the way. "Fucking pigs, I hate chu mothafuckaz! I'm glad your friend got smoked!" He spat with hatred in his eyes and heart. "After I beat this bullshit ass charge, I'ma come looking for your ass, and when I find you I'ma putta bullet in your head, bitch."

Arsenegger spun Puppet around and said, "What did you just say to me?"

"You heard me, cracka mothafucka," he barked.

The crooked badge smiled and licked his lips. He stepped a few feet away from the Vato and cracked off four rounds into his frame, bloodying his white T-shirt. The gunshots rang out in the night startling Mira and Ortiz who was in the process of handcuffing her. Mira screamed and tears flowed freely down her cheeks.

"What the fuck, man?" Ortiz cursed, wearing a shocked expression. He couldn't believe his partner had popped off like that.

Puppet hit the street making a loud thud. He lay on his side with his hands cuffed behind his back gasping for air, as he stared wide eyed at nothing. Arsenegger kneeled down to him and spoke loud enough for just the two of them to hear, "That's for Sullivan. You take one of ours and we'll take one of yours." He pinched his victim's nose closed and held his mouth shut. Hearing Mira still screaming, he yelled to his partner, "Shut that bitch up, will ya?" Ortiz whispered something into Mira's ear, and though she shut up, her body still jerked from trying to hold back her sobbing. Once Puppet wore The Face of Death, Arsenegger un-cuffed him and placed the gun Ortiz found in his car in his hand.

"Great. This is really freaking great." Ortiz said pissed off. "How in the hell are we gonna clean this one up, Einstein?"

"I'll explain everything, now move outta the way." Arsenegger ordered his partner. Ortiz moved from beside Mira leaving her standing alone handcuffed. Her eyes bugged when Arsenegger raised his gun and spat fire at her chest, ripping through her beating heart and spilling her onto the street, dead.

As Arsenegger un-cuffed Mira and placed Ortiz's gun in her hand, he told his partner what they were going to say happened when it came time to fill out the paperwork and do the interview. Unbeknownst to them, somewhere in a window at the top floor of an apartment, behind the shade of a tree was someone filming the entire scenario that took place.

Chapter One

Domino sat behind the Plexiglas in the visiting room watching as his big homeboy, Paybacc, was ushered in by a C.O. Paybacc was a tall, hulk of a man whose body was covered in muscles. He had cold soulless eyes and rope thick dreads that showed signs of graying. He'd been locked up nearly thirteen years for blasting on the police. And although he'd successfully shot one of them he wish he'd killed them both for all of the time he'd gotten.

Paybacc sat his bulky frame down on the tiny stool. For a while he sat there just staring at Domino. Suddenly, he smiled exposing the gold-capped tooth in his grill. Domino managed a weak smile although he had something heavily on his mind. He picked up the telephone and his big homie picked up his.

"What's up with chu, Loco?" Paybacc asked in a husky voice.

"Ain't shit, cuz, just been out here tryna get this money," Domino told him. He was a slender bronze skinned dude. The four moles at the corner of his eye were placed how they'd be on an ivory domino, which was why he'd been given the name.

"I know that's right."

"Who's the lil' homie?" he asked of the brown skinned kid sitting on the stool beside him. His head would have been shaved completely bald if not for the patch of braids at the back of his noggin. The black sunglasses shielded his bloodshot, weed slanted eyes from the world.

"It's me, Wacko, cuz," the youth pulled his sunglasses down.

Paybacc laughed and smiled, "Oh, shit. I remember when you were 'bout yay high. Damn, time flies by, how old are you now, lil' cuz?"

"Nineteen."

"Yeah, cuz is from the hood now." Domino informed.

Paybacc nodded his approval and banged his hood to his heart. Wacko returned the gesture. Paybacc knew the little dude since he was six years old, running around the hood getting into all kinds of mischief. He was given the name Wacko when he shot at a couple of cops with a B.B gun. It was through this act that the homies knew that he either had heart, or was crazy as cat shit. Either way they wanted him down with the set.

"Anyway, what's up in the cold world?" Paybacc switched subjects. Sadden expressions crossed Domino and Wacko's faces and they exchanged glances. And it was from this brief exchange that their OG knew something was wrong. "Domino, what's cracking? This big homie, I need you to be on the up and up." He wore a mask of seriousness as he stared into his little homie's eyes.

Paybacc knew all about the drug war between Nightmare and Pavielle. However, he didn't know Nightmare had been added to the long list of casualties. When Domino told him how Nightmare had been killed, he looked to be unfazed by the news. His only reply was, "I'll be home next week, cuz. Y'all niggaz be ready." He then hung up the telephone and rose to his feet, throwing up his set before being taken away by the C.O.

$$$

Paybacc called for a meeting with the homies in his cell. He informed them of Nightmare's death. The homies got all riled up and vowed to get revenge. Nightmare was widely respected by his neighborhood. He'd devoted his entire life to his set and put in more work than three gangsters combined. He received both fear and respect when he walked the streets and his death brought both grief and relief.

"When I touch the streets these niggaz are gone feel it, cuz. On me," a homie with a jagged scar leading from his ear to his mouth swore, clenching his jaws and balling his fists.

"Nigga, you got five more years before you touchdown," a homie sporting a baldhead reminded him. "It's some Twinkies in the rec room we can smash right now."

"About how many?" Paybacc frowned, placing his hand on baldhead's shoulder.

"Four." Baldhead held up four fingers.

"Fuck we waiting for then?" scarred face asked, cracking his knuckles.

"Y'all go get y'all bangers and meet me back in my house, we're gonna wet these niggaz shirts." Paybacc promised with a screw face.

A few minutes later

The homies entered the rec room with Paybacc bringing up the rear. Slyly, he passed the C.O at the door a hundred dollar bill and he walked off. As soon as the O.G crossed the threshold inside of the recreational room he noticed that the lights were out. The convicts sat quietly watching *The Crow* on TV. Baldhead pointed to the front row where the Bloods were seated. When the convicts saw Paybacc and his homies standing at the door, whispers spread throughout the audience like a plague and one by one the convicts got up and left. Paybacc and the homies swarmed the

Bloods like angry wasps, gripping their lethal weapons tightly. The blue illumination from the television caused their blades to gleam while en route to hand down multiple death sentences. Feeling the aura of a threat approaching, one of the Bloods turned around in his chair. His eyes grew as big as saucers and his mouth formed an O when he saw one of the Crips swinging his shank for his chest.

"Rahhhhhh," He threw his head back roaring like an injured lion, feeling the shank slam into his chest. It was yanked back out and slammed back into him consecutively. Once he toppled over in his chair, the crip straddled his ass and kept putting in that work, speckles of blood clinging to his shirt and face. All hell broke loose as the lights were cut back on. Niggaz were hollering, yelling, and scattering like roaches when the lights came on. The Crips were on their enemies like a pride on gazelles, driving their blades in and out of their bodies. The sound of sharp metal stabbing into flesh was heard along with the bloodcurdling screams of men. One of the Bloods tried to run and was quickly ran down and stabbed with extreme prejudice. Paybacc held one of the Bloods by his throat with an iron grip, his eyes burned with fire as he stared his victim in the eyes.

"This is for Nightmare!" the mountain of muscle grumbled, driving his seven inch ice-pick like shank into the Blood's chest, snapping two of his ribs.

"Ahhhhhhh!" his enemy unleashed a scream so horrible that it caused his attacker's eardrums to ache and tremble. The wounded man's jaw dropped and his eyes bugged as he stared up at his killer. With a grunt, Paybacc drove his shank deeper into the poor bastard's chest, lifting him to the tips of his sneakers. Blood ran from the corner of his mouth and his bottom jaw quivered, slobbering red shit. He stared at Paybacc wide eyed, wondering what he'd done to have such a brutal assault brought against him. The ice-pick was broke off in his chest and he fell to the floor like a ragdoll, bleeding like stuck pig. Paybacc took the time to admire his handiwork before kicking the hell out of the corpse.

"Five Owe, cuz." one of the homie's warned from the door. The mountain of muscle and the homies spilled out of the rec room, leaving three Bloods dead and six others critically injured.

The prison was put on lock-down after the stabbings. And as a result Paybacc was left in his cell with nothing but his thoughts to keep him company. He thought that bringing it to the Bloods would make him feel better, but in all actuality their deaths weren't enough. Gallons upon gallons of blood would have to be spilled before he'd even begin to feel a twinge of satisfaction. When Nightmare was killed he lost a brother, son, and friend all in one. It was something inside of him that wanted him to cry, but the tears wouldn't flow from his eyes. The only emotion he'd ever experienced when dealing with a tragedy was anger. And the only way he could ease the pain was through violence. Harming others was the only thing that made him feel better. It brought him peace.

Lying back in his bunk with his hands clasped behind his head, a devilish smile stretched across Paybacc's face. In seven more days he'd be out on the streets and causing more drama than ever before. He was going to bring hell upon Booby Loco and the Rolling 20s Bloods in the name of his fallen comrade. The heat he'd bring was sure to solidify his legend. He'd be talked about for ages like the old school gangsters before him.

The streets weren't ready, but they had better start preparing for O.G Paybacc's return.

$$$

"No homo, but did you see the size of that mothafucka? He was huge." Wacko exclaimed as he rode in the front passenger seat of Domino's whip. He was speaking on Paybacc's buff neck ass."How much you think cuz benching, 'bout 350, 400?"

Domino shrugged as he guided his '76 Impala S.S through the streets. One hand gripped the steering wheel while the other held the lighter that lit the blunt dangling from the corner of his lips. He took a pull and then blew smoke from his nose and mouth, polluting the air. "It's 'bout to be some shit when that nigga there touches the trenches, you can believe that. If they thought Nightmare was a headache, they for damn sure don't want none of Paybacc." He passed the blunt off to Wacko and shook his head. If all of the streets knew what he knew about his homeboy's return then they asses would go underground.

Wacko took a couple of puffs of the blunt and said, holding the smoke in his lungs, "I've heard some wild stories about cuz while I was coming up. If he's anything like I hear he is, I wouldn't wanna bump shoulders with 'em. Don't get me wrong, I'm not scared of nan nigga out here. I'm just saying, I'd buck his big ass down before I squared up with 'em, ya feel me?"

"I hear you talking." Domino took his hand from the steering wheel to give him a quick pound. "You say you wanna earn a name for yourself, right? Well, hang with me

and the big homie and niggaz will forever remember lil'
Wacko from Gangstas."

Wacko smiled as he thought about the hood stardom
he'd have brushing shoulders with the likes of a gangster of
Paybacc's caliber. True, he was already building quite the
reputation for himself, but doing dirt with Paybacc would
solidify his G status. He couldn't wait until the O.G touched
down so they could tear shit up. Him, Domino, and Paybacc
were gonna be like Three the Hard Way; the Eastside Crips
version.

Chapter Two

As soon as Gangsta stepped out of Wayside County jail he was greeted by the beaming morning sun, his eyes squinting under the intense rays. It was a beautiful day. The sky was a pretty blue. The birds were chirping, and Charles Curtis Vines was a free man. Gangsta closed his eyes and inhaled the fresh outside air. A smile spread across his handsome caramel face. He felt like the luckiest man in the world. He had just beat three murder charges. The D.A had a gun but his finger prints weren't on it, and their confidential informant had turned up dead. With no witness or evidence, Judge Charlene Murdock had no choice but to grant him his walking papers.

When Gangsta opened his eyes there was a white stretch Mercedes Benz before them. Its back door swung open and Bullet stuck his head out and smiled. Gangsta smiled back. "Come on, you free mothafucka!" Bullet waved him over. Gangsta slung his sack of personals over his shoulder and ran for the stretch hog.

Once inside Gangsta exchanged pounds and hugs with Bullet and Black Jesus. Black Jesus pulled out three Cuban cigars; he kept one for himself and gave one to Gangsta and

Bullet. He then produced a Zippo lighter and lit them all. The three men took pulls of their cigars and then blew smoke.

"Cuban, mmmmm," Gangsta said, staring at the cigar. "I thought I'd never taste one of these babies again."

"Welcome home." Black Jesus smiled and nodded.

Gangsta looked to the items beside him. There was a pinstriped suit, a brim, a Franck Muller and gold frames. "Now, this is my style," he said putting on the brim and the frames.

"Now, that you're out, what's the first thing you wanna do?" Black Jesus inquired.

"You mean before you take me to that big welcome home party you planned?" he smiled.

"Yeah, smart ass." The drug lord grinned. "Before that I had a couple of girls lined up. I thought you'd wanna get that eleven month nut off."

"You know I love pussy almost as much as I love money," Gangsta took the cigar from his mouth and thought for a moment. "But I'd really like to stop by the cemetery and visit my family first."

"What cemetery?"

"Inglewood."

"Willie, first stop by Inglewood Cemetery." Black Jesus yelled up front to the chauffer.

"Yes, sir, Mr. Arturo," The African American chauffer replied.

$$$

Gangsta stood before the gravestones of his mother and father. "What's up family? As you know I was down for a minute, but I'm out now. They let your baby boy free, and as soon as I touched down I had Jesus bring me by. I know you guys remember him. We used to come over to the house all the time." He cleared his throat. "Bad news, Booby's laid up in the hospital in a coma. He got into it with this man over…some business. And if he pulls through, he's facing an attempted murder and an illegal firearm charge. The funny thing is the crip that they claimed he was trying to kill, the police winded up killing him. If you wanna know my opinion, I think it's all B.S.

Gouch has gone missing. Some friends of mine have been combing the streets looking for him, but he hasn't turned up. We don't know if he's dead or alive. But we won't stop looking until we find him, tell Robin and Josh they have my word. And as far as me, the institution didn't rehabilitate jack. Either that, or your son is as hardheaded as they come. The streets are all I know, and I'm a die in them doing what I do best." He kneeled down and kissed the black marble gravestones. "I love y'all." He slid on his gold frames and walked toward the stretch white Mercedes Benz that awaited him.

$$$

Hearing knocks at the door; Vayda turned the fire off from under the pan of smothered potatoes and pulled the biscuits from out of the oven, sitting them on top of the stove. She tossed the oven-mitt on top of the counter and headed into the living room. She peeked from behind the curtains through the window and who she saw standing out on her front porch brought a smile to her face. She undid the locks, removed the security chain, and embraced Gangsta.

"When did you get out?" she asked.

"Yesterday, I would have come by, but I had a few things I had to take care of." He said then stood back to take a good look at her. Vayda had cut her hair and had gained a few pounds, but she still looked as beautiful as she did the day he went inside. Gangsta's wondering eyes caused her cheeks to turn red with embarrassment.

"I know you're like damn, this bitch done blew up since I've been gone." Vayda said what she thought was on

O.G's mind as she fidgeted with her fingers. "I've packed up on a few pounds from the baby, but as soon as I push'em out I plan on making the gym my second…"

"Girl, please," he cut her short, waving her off. "Those few lil' pounds did you justice. You look as fine as ever." His compliments caused Vayda to blush. Although Gangsta had a hand in raising Pavielle the Low Bottoms' kingpin didn't possess any of his uncle's smoothness and charm. Vayda understood why he was considered a ladies' man; it was something about him that pulled women in like quicksand. With his swagger and gift of gab in another life he could have been a pimp.

"Thanks," Vayda tried to conceal her smile.

"I see y'all beefed up the home security." Gangsta commented on the Muslim brothers posted up outside. He was immediately searched and relieved of his weapon as soon as he crossed the threshold into the yard. It wasn't until he made the one in charge put in a call to his cousin Lenny Jihad that his weapon was given back, and he was allowed to enter the house.

"Yeah, Pavy had your cousin Lenny send a few of his guys over to guard the house." Vayda informed him.

"Some of those cats are old school playaz." Gangsta said. "One of the cats out there, Ross, cut a dude's throat from ear to ear for cheating in a card game. I don't know what kind of dream Farrakhan selling, but it must be a damn good one to get that brotha there to flip."

"It's nice to know I'm in caring hands." Vayda said sarcastically. "I was just in the middle of making breakfast, you want a plate?"

"Nah, but I'll take a cup of coffee." Gangsta approached the sofa. "Who you got over here sleeping on the job?" he slowly began to peel the blanket back.

"Oh, that's Killa Dre."

Gangsta froze when he felt the barrel of a weapon press against his manhood.

"I'm never asleep on the job," Killa Dre claimed. He had scum in his eyes and white stuff at the corners of his mouth. He was a light sleeper, and in his slumber he could hear a pin drop on cotton. The young nigga cracked a smile and Gangsta cracked one back.

"That's right. Can't catch my young nigga slipping," Gangsta slapped hands with the young boy.

"And you know this." Killa Dre threw the blanket off his person and sat up. He sat the silver revolver, which he'd pressed into Gangsta's crotch, on the coffee-table and sat his M-16 rifle against the sofa. "Yo, sis, can you fix me a cup of black coffee, please?" he asked heading toward the backroom.

"Sure." Vayda responded from over her shoulder, preparing a pot of coffee.

Killa Dre returned to the living room wiping his face with a washcloth and sat down on the sofa. Vayda entered the living room with two cups of coffee and later two plates of food for she and Killa Dre.

"When was the last time you went to see Booby?" Gangsta asked seriously from the La-Z-Boy.

"A few days ago, I wanted to stay but the cop watching his door wasn't having it." Vayda informed him. "They have him under watchful eyes until he wakes up outta that coma, and when he does they're gonna usher right off to county to begin trial on that illegal weapon charge."

"I gotta get up there to see my nephew and make sure he's OK. I trust those pigs as far as I can see'em." Gangsta said, remembering when Detective Arsenegger threatened to kill his entire family and anyone associated with them. He'd never tell Vayda that though. The girl was already on edge with her fiancé being laid up in the hospital on the brink of death. "Y'all got any word on Gucci yet?"

"Notta word," Vayda replied, biting into a crisp strip of bacon.

"Man, it's like Gucci fell off the face of the planet, Blood. No one has seen or heard from him since the Mexicans raided the spot." Killa Dre took a sip of his black coffee. Recalling something, he snapped his fingers. "Oh, that's what I've been meaning to tell you."

"What's up?" Gangsta sat his coffee on the coffee-table and removed his suit's coat. He then leaned forward and listened attentively to his little homie.

"A few of the homies got whacked and the others are laying up in the infirmary up there." Killa Dre told him. "Word is some crabs got'em. The homies are saying it was some O.G nigga named Paybacc and a few others fools that did'em in."

"Paybacc? Are you sure?"

"Yep, Paybacc; I remember specifically, but who the fuck is he? Niggaz acting like he's the Boogeyman or some shit."

In all of his years in the life Gangsta had never met a man quite like Paybacc. He believed that if the Devil walked this earth he was surely using O.G killer's body as his vessel. Paybacc was the meanest son of a bitch to have ever oozed out from between a woman's legs. The horrible acts he committed would have him talked about for decades to come like the noted tragedy of 9/11. Paybacc was already a headache for his peers, but once he'd gotten shot and lived to tell the tale, he was hell on wheels. He brought a whole new meaning to the term wicked once he'd gotten released from County General. When he couldn't find the cat that put seven holes in him, he rode on the enemies that were familiar to his set until he felt better.

Gangsta remembered the summer of '93 all too well. The temperatures reached a scorching ninety seven degrees but Paybacc made it even hotter. Gangsta lost many homies on the account of Paybacc delivering on the definition of his name. He was hurt about losing his comrades but mad at his self for not finishing Paybacc off when he caught him slipping in The World on Wheels parking lot. He thought that seven shots would be enough to send the O.G crip on a vacation to Satan's house, but he was dead wrong, and his homies would be the ones to pay the price.

"You know that fool got locked up a few years back for blasting on Binem, right?" Gangsta asked. "He got thirteen years so he should be touching down in a minute, and when he does he's gonna want some get-back for Nightmare. Old boy was like his lil' brotha, so you know he feels some type of way about his passing."

Killa Dre munched on his food and sucked his fingers. He then wiped his hands with a napkin, balled it up, and dropped it into his plate. "I'm not stunting this nigga, Blood. If he sleeps, eats, shits and came outta pussy like we did, then he can hurt and bleed like us, too. Feel me? These niggaz out here aren't invincible. Shit, even Superman died."

Gangsta nodded his head and massaged his chin. "We're gonna deal with Paybacc and the rest of these niggaz accordingly. We're gonna smash their set so hard that they'll think twice about rolling back on us."

Killa Dre smiled wickedly and rubbed his hands together. "That's what I'm talking about, it's been a minute since yo' Y.G been on the frontline, when you talking about shooting this movie?"

"Soon, real soon," he assured him.

Chapter Three

Gouch's eyes fluttered opened and he sat up in bed. Looking around he realized he was in a basement of some facility. Pieces of paper littered the floor. There were news paper clippings on the wall along with pictures that were hung up by thumbtacks. A stained tan sofa, a wooden chair with a flower print cushion covered by plastic, and a battered nightstand, which sat in the far corner were the only pieces of furniture. A *Beeping* sound drew Gouch's attention to his left where he discovered a heart monitor and a couple of other machines. He saw that the cords and tubes running from them were attached to his body.

Pulling the tubes and cords from his form, Gouch noticed that his hand was wrapped in an Ace-Bandage. He un-wrapped his hand and saw that it was burned to the point where it resembled barbequed rib meat. Feeling tightness around his crown, he touched his head and felt the texture of more Ace-Bandages. Across the room there was a fingerprint stained full body mirror that was broken at the corner. He threw the blankets off of his person and rushed over to it. He couldn't see himself in it so he spat on it and used his forearm to rub out a clear circle where he could see his reflection. He then, as quickly as he possible, un-wrapped his noggin and revealed the severe burns he sustained. His left ear was mangled and the side of his face was partially burned. He pulled off his wife-beater and tossed it aside. The burn scars were down his arm and covered part of his back. He brought his fingers over his wounds feeling them as if they were Braille. In doing so he remembered the night he was given the scars. Some Mexicans had raided the trap house spraying shit up. They didn't even say shit, they just busted in the house blasting. He'd lost quite a few homies that night: Debo, Neck Bone, and Ridah Man. The only ones alive were himself and Killa Dre. He'd sent the young boy to the liquor store to cop some swishers before the Mexicans hit the trap. So he was pretty sure he was alive.

The night the Mexicans hit was a crazy one. Slugs were flying every which way with Gouch ducking and dodging them, trying to avoid catching one in his ass. The last thing he remembered was running upstairs to get Big Boy out of the closet: his M-16 assault rifle. He was popping off at the mouth and dumping slugs at the same time. He figured if he was going to go out then he was going to have his enemies lying in body bags beside him. Gouch was prepared to go out in ablaze and die a gangsta's death. He thought his enemies bullets would be his undoing, but instead it came in the form of a hand grenade. The damn thing caught him by surprise. He tried to run but ended up getting caught by the blast. Everything went black and he went tumbling down to the foot of the stairs. When he began to come to he saw a bunch of cops standing in the living room. He knew there was no way he could explain all the hammers and dope he'd stashed in the basement so he got ghost. He recalled staggering down San Pedro before collapsing in an alley.

Gouch leaned forward looking closer into his reflection. He didn't like what he saw staring back at him. He looked like some sort of circus freak. He was hideous. He was a monster. He was ugly. Now his inside matched his outside. Gouch punched the mirror causing it to crack into a cobweb. Pulling his fist back he noticed tiny cuts and licked them like a thirsty kitten. He heard barking dogs and the shuffling of feet as someone came through the basement door. Whoever it was had started in his direction, Gouch could tell by the echoes his boots made on the floor. His footfalls seemed to grow closer as they moved in his direction. Gouch went to grab his twin Berettas from his waistline and came up with air. He lifted his shirt and inspected his waistband and found it naked. A confused expression crossed his face and he realized he'd lost his babies when he was caught in the explosion. He looked across the room and spotted a barrel of wooden boards. He went to dash over and tripped over a dog's chew toy, landing on his side and grimacing.

"Son of a bitch," He bawled, holding his ribs. A trio of dogs consisting of a Bulldog, a Labrador Retriever and a Rottweiler surrounded him barking and licking his face. A shadow eclipsed Gouch's form and his eyes popped open. They found an old light skinned man with an unkempt beard before them. He mirrored the rapper Ice-T. He held a long wooden stick which he used to support his weight. His nappy locks spilled from under a Dodgers cap that looked like it had seen its fair share of heads. A beaded necklace that held onto a pendant that was the continent of Africa hung from his neck. He filled out a faded The Simpsons T-shirt, which he wore a hefty black jacket over. The brown boots that graced his feet were old and looked like rotten potatoes.

The old man stood there staring at Gouch for a time before he outstretched a gloved hand. Gouch looked from the gloved hand to the eyes of the man it belonged to. He couldn't make them out because they were beneath black sunglasses.

"Take it." The old man said of his hand. Gouch reached out and the old man pulled him to his feet. The old man turned his back on him and went off into a corner where he rummaged in a couple of boxes. "Can I interest you in a cup of tea and some Fig Newton's?"

"Hell yeah, I'm starving." Gouch winced as he rubbed his aching side.

"Figure you'd say as much, you've been out for quite some time."

"What's your name, old timer?"

"Shelly. And I don't know why, you'd have to dig up my mother and ask her yourself." He said of his feminine name. He filled a pot with bottle water and sat it on a single electrical burner, turning it on. He then went about the task of feeding his dogs.

"Where are we?" Gouch's eyes took a tour of the basement.

"We're in the basement of an old medical supply warehouse, but I like to call it home." He hung up his Dodger cap and his jacket. "I found you passed out in an alley. You were a sight to see with all of that blood covering you. I thought you'd bought the farm until I checked your pulse. I dug as much of that shrapnel outta ya as I could before I sewed ya back up. I used some of the equipment I had lying around here to monitor your vitals, so I'd know ya were still alive. I bathed ya and clothed ya. Hell, I even changed your diaper when you shat yourself." He chuckled, showcasing his rotten and missing teeth. Gouch frowned and checked his sweats, discovering that he was wearing Depends.

"Thanks. But why not save yourself the trouble and take me to a hospital?" Gouch asked curiously.

"Because helping people is what I do," Shelly said, pouring a cup of tea. "I'm in the business of saving lives. Besides, if we don't take care of our own, then who will?"

"How long have I been down here?"

Shelly's response was throwing a Los Angeles Times news paper at him. Gouch scanned the paper for a date and he found it: September 15th 2012. He plopped down on the bed and tossed the news paper aside. He brought a palm down his mug and blew hard.

"I've been out for a day." He said to himself.

"Yep," Shelly brought Gouch his cup of tea and a few Fig Newton bars.

Shelly sipped his cup of tea and watched as Gouch tore into the Fig Newton bars. He crammed the bars into his mouth and scoffed them down hungrily. The way he was munching on them you'd think he'd be lynched if he were caught eating them. He picked up the cup of tea and before he could take a sip, Shelly said, "Be easy now, it's hot."

Gouch ignored Shelly's warning and proceeded to drink the tea without caution: big mistake. The hot, brown liquid scolded his tongue and mouth, he spat it out. "Ahhhhhh, shit!" he bellowed.

"Told ya," Shelly grinned and sipped his tea. Gouch wiped his mouth with the back of his hand and the old man noticed the tattoo on his forearm: Rolling 20s. "What's your name, son?"

"Gouch, but chu can call me, Gucci." He said, trying to sip the tea this time.

"I mean the name you were given at birth, the one that's on your California I.D."

"Gregory."

"Hmmmm, Gregory." Shelly nodded. "It's a hell of a lot better than Shelly."

"Yeah, all the tough guy names were taken."

"Are you a gangbanger, Gregory?" Sipping his tea with one hand, Gouch used his freehand to throw up his hood, "The Eastside Outlaws Rolling Twenties, huh? I'm familiar. Tell me, how many men have you killed, Gregory?"

"I've never killed anyone in my life."

"Then what's this?" Shelly pointed to the red tattooed tears at the corner of Gouch's right-eye. "I'm notta square; I was running these streets when you were just an itch in your daddy's pants. I know what that ink means, son."

"Yeah, I gangbang, but who doesn't? This is L.A, pops, I don't know where you from, but out here it's the way of the land. Besides, I was born into this shit. It ain't like a nigga had too many options."

"Poor lil' ghetto boy, save me the sob stories 'cause I've heard them all. Hell, I got plenty of my own." Gouch waved him off. "You're a killer, and you wear that shit like a badge of honor." He shook his head shamefully.

"You're mothafucking right." Gouch said proudly.

Shelly sat his cup of tea down and walked over to Gouch. "I bet all those men you killed were black, weren't they? Young brothers that look like you and me; came from the same struggle as you and I. Go ahead Badass, tell me I'm lying." The lanky gangbanger looked away in shame. It was true. The old man had hit the nail on the head. All the men Gouch had pushed into a grave were African American men just like he and Shelly. He had never thought about it that way though. When he was loading up his Berettas it was to defend and protect his hood. He didn't look at the men before his guns as his own; to him they were the enemy. "That's what I thought."

"Blood, fuck this, I don't have to listen to this shit." Gouch spat and slid his bare feet into his sneakers, making for the door. Shelly tapped the floor with his stick and his dogs ran over to the doorway, blocking Gouch's path. The dogs bared their canines, barking and snarling at the man that was standing before them trying to leave. Lines formed across Gouch's forehead, It was eerie to him how the animals went from loving pooches to vicious guard dogs at the tap of their master's stick.

Gouch looked around for a weapon and spotted an old wooden bat amongst a pile of junk. He started for it and was tripped up by Shelly's stick. He spilled awkwardly to the floor and landed on his back wincing. He went to get up and met a hard strike to the chin that knocked him out cold. Shelly tapped the floor with his stick and the Rottweiler drug Gouch by the collar of his hospital gown beside the bed. He tapped the floor once more and the Bulldog and Labrador retriever delivered him a rusted chain and shackle. Shelly attached one end of the chain to a radiator and tugged on it, testing it stability. He then clamped the metal-bracelet around Gouch's ankle.

"There ya go." Shelly patted him on the head. He then pulled up a chair and grabbed a bottle of Brandy from off his cluttered desk. He removed the cap and took a long guzzle. When he brought the bottle down he found his dogs staring at him and licking their chops. "I guess you fellas do deserve a taste. Spartacus," he called the Bulldog. "fetch your bowl." The Bulldog retrieved his dog bowl and Shelly poured some for the threesome. He then took the occasional swig from the bottle while watching the dogs drink from the bowl.

These were man's best friends.

Chapter Four

Nightmare's funeral fell on a warm Sunday afternoon. The whole ceremony took place inside of his mother's home. There were gangsters that no one had seen since the birth of the set coming out of the woodworks to pay their respect to the fallen soldier. When the attendees entered through the door of Mrs. Grant's home they were expecting to find an open coffin with the deceased lying inside at peace, but instead they found Nightmare standing on his own two feet. His corpse looked like a wax figure standing in his mother's living room. His face wore a mad dog stare and his eyes were covered by black sunglasses. His hair was parted into squares with small afro puffs coming out of them. He stood with his heels touching each other creating half of the number four, with his fingers twisted up representing his set. A gold chain hung from his neck with a charm that was two pool balls of the numbers that his neighborhood represented. He was fitted in a navy blue silk shirt and slacks.

A pearl white Yukon truck pulled in front of Nightmare's mother's house, grasping the attention of the people gathered outside of the packed house that the funeral was taking place. The passenger side door of the hog flew open and Paybacc placed his black leather, hard bottom shoe onto the pavement and pulled himself into view. The shocks of the SUV cried out in relief as the massive man removed his six foot two, two-hundred and fifty pound frame from its confines. His thick locks were snugly tucked underneath a gray skully. His dark eyes were hidden behind gold frames with black lenses. His broad chest stretched the fabric of a white V-neck T-shirt, which was under the suit jacket of a gray two piece suit that hugged his tree trunk like arms and legs like a latex glove. His hand held onto the passenger door as he gave a quick scan of the many faces of the people whose attention he'd garnered. It wasn't until Domino and Wacko were at his side that he closed the door and began his journey through the yard. At first there were hard stares, and then came the whispers of those present. He could hear his name being uttered amongst his audience and soon some of the hard faces had softened to more pleasant ones. It was evident that his legacy had captured the men and women present like a magic trick.

Paybacc made his way towards Mrs. Grant's house slapping hands with the folks he knew and ignoring the cold stares of the ones he wasn't familiar with. There were quite a few new faces in the crowd; teenagers and kids barely out of grade school that were now from a hood he'd been representing for the past thirty something years. He couldn't help but to think how younger the bangers were getting with each generation. Crossing the threshold into the house, he could hear the wails of the minister as he delivered his sermon. Beads of sweat rolled from his balding scalp and over his puffy brown cheeks. The more he went on the more Mrs. Grant, who was wrapped in her daughter, Shantel's arms, sobbed. A light skinned man in a cream V-neck sweater and jeans was seated beside her with his arm draped over a crying little boy's shoulder. The light skinned man wiped the boy's face with a tissue and kissed him on the side of his head. Paybacc remembered the twosome from a picture Shantel had sent him while he was locked up. They were Trevor and Dontai Jr., her son and her uncle.

When Mrs. Grant looked over her shoulder and saw Paybacc she rose to her feet and rushed over to him, wrapping her arms around him. She sobbed into the torso of his suit as he rubbed her back, comforting her. He hated that she'd decided to use his $3,000 dollar Armani suit as a Kleenex, but he didn't have the heart to pull her away.

With a tear streaked face, Shantel looked over to the mountain of muscle, smiled weakly, and waved. He did the same.

At the repast homies were eating, smoking, drinking and shooting the shit. Domino took the time to bring Paybacc up to speed on the happenings in the hood and introduced him to their newest recruits as well as some of their stalwart soldiers. Most of them heard about Paybacc's exploits but they had never met him. Realizing they had a live and in the flesh legend in their presence caused them turn into groupies. And more than a handful were dick riding the O.G. Paybacc couldn't help but smile because not too long ago it was these same cats that were giving him the evil eye. Now they'd turned into a couple of crazed fans meeting the lead guitarist of a Rock & Roll band.

Later that night Paybacc found himself kicking amongst his comrades old and new, he took a few more puffs of a blunt before passing it off to one of his homeboys. He then grabbed his suits' jacket and made to head into the house.

"Where you going, cuz?" one of the homies asked.

"To pay the water bills, I'll be right back." Paybacc said over his shoulder.

Paybacc heard the cries of a woman as he moved through the hallway. He doubled back to the cracked open door of a bedroom he'd passed and peeked inside. He found Mrs. Grant sitting on the bed staring at a portrait of her family. Hot tears rolled down her face and splashed on the glass of the frame. She sniffled and wiped her eyes with a tissue.

"Are you all right?" Paybacc asked as he entered the bedroom and sat beside her. An honest expression of concern was across his face.

"Oh, hey, Clifton," she sat the portrait on the dresser. "I'm OK."

"You sure, can I get chu something?" Paybacc rubbed her back to sooth her.

"No, I'm alright," she managed a weak smile, but it gave way to tears. "Oh, why do I keep saying that? I'ma total mess! I'ma complete wreck! I don't know what I'm going to do! I just lost my baby boy. I keep pinching myself hoping that I'll wake up and this will all have been a nightmare." She turned to Paybacc, and for the first time, he saw her bloodshot and puffy eyes. His heart went out to her, he couldn't have imagined how it must have felt to lose a child, and he hoped that he never would. "After his father was murdered I thought I'd never get over his death, but eventually I did. But this is different, this is my baby." The tears ran and she dabbed them away with her tissue. "Boy, who am I kidding? I knew this was coming one day, especially with David. We all knew David was no angel, notta angel of God, at least. But still he was my little boy and I loved him with all of my heart." She shook her head. "Look at me sitting up here…I got the nerve to cry. There's no telling how many mothers my son has put in this predicament. How many wives has David made widows? How many children have been left fatherless because of him? Those people had their turns to grieve and now it's mine. I see it now; this is God's way of punishing me for bringing such a monster into this world."

"Hush, momma," Shantel said from the doorway where she held a Newport 100 pinched between her fingers. Her eyes were still puffy from crying but she was done with grieving, at least for the time being she was. "God is not punishing you. What happened to my brother was karma; what goes around comes around. David done dirt and dirt got done to him. The game these young black men are out here playing is cut throat, and these niggaz know that before they get into it, but that doesn't deter them."

"You can look at it your way, but I'll look at it mine." Mrs. Grant replied and wiped her nose with the tissue. "Let me get one of those cancer-sticks." She held the cigarette between her lips while her daughter lit it for her. She took a pull and then blew the smoke out into the air.

"Momma, you give Clifton what David left him yet?" Shantel asked.

Mrs. Grant smacked her forehead. "Damn, I forgot."

"What is it?" Paybacc's forehead creased with wonderment, watching Mrs. Grant rummage through her closet.

"Got it," she smiled when she produced a video-tape.

"What's on the tape?"

"I don't know, but apparently David made it before he died." She told him. "I was told it was for your eyes only." Mrs. Grant popped the video cassette into the VCR and hit the POWER button. "Come on, let's give'em some privacy." She led Shantel out of the bedroom and closed the door shut behind them.

The "40 inch flat-screen was filled with static for a moment, and then Nightmare appeared lounging in a black leather executive chair smoking a blunt.

"What's cracking, cuz? Welcome home, Eastside," Nightmare spoke, eyes hooded from the pontent weed his was smoking on. "I got something for you, loved one...think of it as a homecoming present. Pull that chest out of mom's closet; the combination is our hood day," Paybacc pulled the chest out of the closet and put in the combination. He undone the locks and raised the lid to reveal blocks of Benjamin Franklins wrapped in plastic. Paybacc picked up one of the blocks and tested its weight, bouncing it up and down in the palm of his hand. "I already took care of moms and big sis, so that's all you," Paybacc dropped the block back inside of the chest and shut it, sitting down on it. "Well, if you're seeing this that means they've finally got my ass. Niggaz finally managed to smoke The Loc, and that ain't an easy task. Anyway, you've been down with the set since before I was born. And I can't think of a more real, more standup cat to lead the hood in my passing, except for my old head, the gangsta that put me on to this game and showed me what cripping is all about. The crown is all yours, and you have my blessings." He mashed the blunt out in the ashtray and sat up, interlocking his fingers. "All I ask is that you do me a solid, cuz. Find that nigga Booby Loc and make him suffer, and just when he's had enough suffering and he can't take no more, make him suffer some more before you slit his fuking throat." He pretended to cut his throat with his thumb, dragging it around his neck. "I want him and everyone that's got love for him dead. Ain't no love for the other side, fuck them pricks. Salute," He threw up his set. "I'm out. Burn this tape."

Paybacc ejected the video-tape and stuffed it at the small of his back. He'd begun the task of locking the chest when someone knocked at the door.

"Who is it?" he called out.

"Shantel." she answered.

"Come in."

Shantel stepped inside with a long sack slung over her shoulder loaded with weapons. "This is something else David wanted you to have." She handed the sack over to Paybacc.

"Thanks, sis, could you tell Domino and Wacko to come here for a sec, please?"

"Alright," She pulled the door closed.

Paybacc emptied the contents of the sack onto the bed. Scattered before him were a number of guns ranging from handguns to assault rifles. He picked up a two Tec-9s and envisioned himself dumping on the enemies he'd accumulated over the years.

"Goddamn!" Domino said, seeing the guns. He and Wacko had just entered the bedroom.

"Y'all close the door; I don't want everybody in my business." Paybacc told them.

Domino closed the door and picked up a MP-5 while Wacko grabbed an AR-18. They envisioned themselves blazing at their enemies just as Paybacc had.

"Nightmare left you these?" Wacko asked.

"Yeah, he asked that I put'em to good use, too. So you know what that means."

"Killing season, my gangstas," Domino said, bug eyed and licking his lips. The expression on his face was a mixture of excitement and insanity. It was something about doing dirt that gave him a high that no drug could ever mimic.

Wacko glanced at the chest. "What's in the chest?"

Paybacc stepped in front of Wacko's view of the chest holding the Tec-9s. "Why are you so nosey, cuz?" his face twisted, he hated a mothafucka that didn't mind his own business.

"My bad," Wacko went back to toying with the AR-18.

"There's something I think y'all should see." Paybacc whipped out the video-tape.

$$$

"Okilla, cuz, y'all listen up," Domino said from the top of a garage rooftop, overlooking a sea of his homeboys and homegirls. The backyard was cramped with so many crips that if he fell he'd be forever lost amongst his audience. Domino had called the meeting to deliver some news that would alter how the Eastside Crips operated as a gang.

Hearing the bass in Domino's voice made the audience settle down from their chit chatter and give him their undivided attention. "As y'all already know, the Twinkies killed Taco and Nightmare about a week ago. Before the homie got bodied he said the leadership of the set was to be given to…" Domino's eyes looked over the faces of his audience; they were all staring into his mouth in anticipation of the new shot-caller's name. "O.G Paybacc," The audience erupted in applause. Domino stepped aside and Paybacc stepped forth. He removed his gold frames and allowed his eyes to sweep back and forth across his sea of comrades. A mesh of the audiences voices came together and they all pumped their fists into the air, chanting his name as if he was some kind of gladiator that had just slaughtered his opponent in cold blood.

Chapter Five

"So, you've been holding us down since Booby got laid up and Gucci went missing, huh?" Gangsta asked as he maneuvered his black-on-black F-150 on chrome 28s through the streets. Killa Dre nodded. He stared out the window watching the blur of the city as the truck sped through The City of Angels. "I admire that, a young nigga like you taking care of grown man business; respect."

"We're all crew. I'm just doing my part, feel me?" Killa Dre replied.

"So, who are the new niggaz you put under our umbrella?"

"Banga, Playboy, Bourne and Mad Man," Killa Dre told him. "They all got their lil' spots andworkers. But everyone reports to me and I take in that money at the end of the night. I hit the workers with their due, give Vayda her taste and I stash the rest away for Booby for when he comes outta coma."

"Young boss in training. How old are you now, Dre?"

"I turned seventeen last month." He said, taking the cigarette from behind his ear and the red lighter from his pocket. He was about to light up when he stopped and looked to Gangsta. "You mind if I put the fire to this cancer-stick?"

"Nah, go ahead." Gangsta rolled up all of the windows so the wind wouldn't blow out the flame of the young nigga'z lighter while he was lighting the cigarette. Once the youth was done he let the windows back down.

"How has your mother been doing? I mean, with the passing of your brother and all?"

Killa Dre blew smoke and said, "She cries a lot. The walls at our house are paper thin, so I can hear her through them. In the morning she dances around in the kitchen singing and cooking breakfast how she use to before Mel got killed, like everything is copasetic. I guess she's trying to put up a front for me, but I see right through her. Right now she's fragile. She's just barely holding on to her sanity, but if something was to happen to me, I know it would be the last straw."

"What did she say about the graffiti?" Gangsta inquired about the tattoos on his little homie's face.

Killa Dre shook his head and said, "Same thing she said about me dropping out of school: nothing. She just took me by the face and stared into my eyes. It was kind of weird. I guess she was looking to see if there were any traces of her lil' man left. Andre Johnson is long gone. He died alongside his big brother. They buried him and he can never come back, Blood."

Killa Dre's big brother played football for Jefferson high school. He was said to have been one of the best running backs in the county. He had big dreams and a promising future with scouts looking to draft him, but all of that came to a tragic end when he was murdered in a revenge shooting. Tramel was gangbanging, he was simply caught at the wrong place at the wrong time.

The loss of his brother had taken its toll on Killa Dre. He'd gotten drunk and high out of his mind many nights, cursing God and swearing revenge. He got it too. Killa Dre tracked his brother's killer, Reboc, down to an apartment building out in The Junglez where he was laying low after catching the body. It was there that he put him to sleep forever.

"Well, at least something good came outta my conversion and my brother's death; I can keep a decent roof over our heads, food on the table, and the lights on. Shit, I'm only fifteen and I'm making more money than a lotta these grown working mothafuckaz." He took a hit of his cigarette.

Gangsta nodded his head. "True. But let me ask you this…is your paper being longer worth your lifespan being shorter?"

Killa Dre took the time to think on it. "If my death means a better life for my family, then I'd gladly lay in a coffin."

"You know what chu sound like right now?"

"What?"

"A man."

Killa Dre smirked and took a pull from his cigarette.

Gangsta spotted some hardheads hanging around a liquor store. He could tell by the way they were strategically posted that they were slinging. The lookout was on the corner, the slinger was in front of the store, and the cat holding the gun stood on the other side of the store.

"Look at these niggaz; they're out here slipping like bare feet on an ice block." Gangsta said, giving his observation. "My nephew is laid up and they think shit don't stink. I'ma 'bout to shake these pussies up," He looked to Killa Dre. "You got your heater on you?"

"You finna wash them niggaz, Blood?" Killa Dre asked, pulling his burner off his waistline and handing it to him.

"Nah, I'm just about to rattle their nerves," Gangsta executed the headlights of his truck and eased up the street. Seeing the SUV creeping up caused the trio to freeze in place. They didn't know if it was enemies, or some nigga that was coming through to stunt in his new toy. Their heads were on swivels as they watched the car get closer and closer. Gangsta stopped in front of the store and smiled devilishly as he swung the gun around and out of the window. "Rolling!" he bellowed, cracking off three rounds that caused the threesome to scramble like a bag of marbles being emptied on the floor. Gangsta blew out the back and side windows of a parked Saturn, deliberately missing the men standing out front hustling. He and Killa Dre sped off laughing so hard that tears formed at the corners of their eyes.

"Did you see them niggaz, man?" Killa Dre asked coming down from his laughter.

"Did I?" Gangsta said, wiping the corners of his eyes. "This game ain't for everybody, baby boy."

$$$

The shutter of the storage unit squealed as Killa Dre lifted it from the floor. Once Gangsta walked inside, he closed the shutter down back. Gangsta looked over the unit. There was furniture and boxes scattered everywhere.

"I had to dress things up a bit to throw The Ones off in case they get the idea to come snooping around." Killa Dre informed him.

"Whose name is this place under?" Gangsta asked, looking through a couple of boxes.

"It's under a dummy: Benson Doherty." Killa Dre answered. He flipped over a couch, kneeled down, and pulled the cloth from the bottom of it. He started pulling out blocks of cocaine that were wrapped in Saran Wrap and had an image of a Black Jesus Christ stamped on them. "This is how much work I got left." He stood erect looking the blocks of cocaine over.

Gangsta counted the blocks of cocaine with his foot and slid them aside. There were a total of eight. He flipped the couch back over, stacked the blocks up, and sat them on the couch. "Is this me?" he asked Killa Dre of the eight blocks of cocaine.

"Nah, that's Booby's shit." he told him. He was standing beside a deep freezer holding its lid open. "We burned through all of your coke." He motioned Gangsta over. Gangsta stepped forth and poked his head inside the deep freezer. The deep freezer was filled with $10,000 dollar stacks. "That's three mill, easy. You can run it through the counter, I got one stashed in the box labeled kitchen appliances."

"I'ma do that at the house, throw the lock back on that bitch. I'ma see about getting someone to pick up this coke. I'll help you throw this deep freezer in the back of the truck and you can push it back to the house. I'll catch a cab. A FED bust me with three mill and eight of them thangs, he's liable to cum in his pants." Gangsta whipped out his cell and placed a few calls. Once he was done he slid the cell back inside of his suit. He hopped upon the deep freezer and took a glance at his Franck Muller.

Killa Dre sat on the arm of the couch. "You ever think about what you'll do if Booby doesn't come outta his coma?"

"He will."

"But what if he doesn't?"

"I never thought about that." Gangsta said, staring at nothing. Booby's situation was serious, and if he didn't pull through then he would have to start back running his empire. Although he wanted to be back on the throne, he didn't want it to come at this cost.

Chapter Six

"So what's up with this clown that popped Nightmare?" Paybacc asked as he dipped his hand into an aquarium and pulled out his pet python. The dread lock rocking killer acquired the serpent not long after he'd touchdown in the hood. Paybacc gently stroked the snake as he carried him over to the couch and propped his feet upon the coffee-table.

"Nigga laid up in County, man. He's in a coma. The boys are watching over him so there ain't no way we can touch 'em." This was Domino. He was leaning against the stove with his arms folded to his chest and chewing on a Twizzler.

"Nightmare gave 'em two before One Time punched his clock in," Wacko added from where he was sitting on the loveseat flipping through cable channels. "Who knows? He may check out and save us the bullets."

"And he and Nightmare's beef was behind drugs?" Paybacc's forehead crinkled.

"Yep," Domino confirmed, "Booby was cutting in on Nightmare's business. He was losing money. Booby was serving up a product that was A1; mothafucking fiends gave his work two thumbs up. All of the heads started going to the other side to get their blasts. Nightmare came up with a solution: eliminate the competition and take the whole shit back over again. To make a long story short, we locked ass with the slobs. We lost some and they lost some, but in the end they winded up getting one up on us with the homie's death."

"One up on us?" Wacko looked at Domino like. "We lost Reboc, Nike, Supacrip, C-note, Crow, and O.G Cas; not to mention some of our Tiny Locs. The Twinks were kicking our asses."

"Don't wet it, Loco. I'm here to make amends." Paybacc assured him, leaning back *Keep it real* staring the python in its eyes and watching its tongue slither in and out of its mouth. "Now, tell me what chu know about this prick. Who is his family? Who is he close with?"

"He has a preggo fiancé, her name is Vayda." Domino informed him.

"You're talking about that lil' red bitch? That broad bad than a mothafucka, I'd dick her down raw." Wacko smiled, revealing his crooked and bunched teeth.

"You ain't saying shit, I done seen you dick some smoker bitches down raw. Old dirty dick nigga." Wacko shrugged. "Sometimes I wonder if you're crazy, or just stupid playing Russian roulette with your life." Domino looked at his little homie like he was an idiot and shook his head. "Anyway, cuz," he addressed Paybacc. "Booby has an older brother named Gouch, but he's M.I.A, don't nobody know where this nigga at. He just disappeared a couple of days ago. Then there's his uncle Gangsta who just got outta the pen. He's an O.G nigga. A real reputable from what I understand. He's from your era, so I figured you'd probably be familiar with him."

"Yeah, I know who he is." Paybacc confirmed, allowing the python to slither from around his neck and up his arm. "If my memory serves me correct, he was more of a hustla than a killa. Still, I wouldn't take him lightly. He done put in his work and earned his stripes."

There was a knock at the door that swept the living room with silence. Paybacc and Wacko drew their weapons and pointed them at the door. Domino waved his hand signaling for them to put their burners away. "Man, put them thangz away before y'all scare off the hoes I invited over here." He told them and they obliged.

"Man, you didn't tell me you were inviting some jumps over," Wacko said. "I would have got some sticky and some drank."

"Easy, dick; these skeezas aren't for us," Domino told him. "They're for the big homie, cuz."

"For me? You shouldn't have," Paybacc asked with a hand to his chest grinning.

Domino chuckled and said, "I figured you'd wanna empty that thirteen years worth of semen you got clogging your pipe, cuz."

"That's love, Loco. Now, open the door for the hoes, you can't keep the bitches waiting." He hurried Domino along.

Domino pulled open the door and stepped aside so the ladies could enter. The first one through the door was a tall and slender honey with golden brown skin and burgundy twisties that she wore pulled back in a ponytail. The second chick was thick with a chocolate complexion. She had full lips and dark almond eyes. Most men claimed she looked like the porn star Beauty Dior.

Domino closed and locked the door, then stood beside the girls. Smiling and rubbing his hands together, he said, "Paybacc, meet Passion and Traquila. Passion and Traquila, meet my big homie Paybacc. He just came home." He introduced them.

"What's cracking?" Paybacc threw his head back like *What's up?* He approached to shake Passion's hand and she stepped back, afraid of the python.

"Does he bite?" Passion asked.

Paybacc looked to the python then to Passion. "Yeah, this snake bites, but this one don't." he shook the bulge in his jeans at the girls. Both their eyes bugged having been impressed by his size. The thickest girl licked her top lip and having done so exposed the stud in her tongue. She eyed the O.G's package hungrily. Her nipples hardened and showed through her wife-beater and she felt her coochie ooze with moisture. She'd found herself growing horny just thinking about Paybacc's pole splitting her bald sex. She glanced over at her homegirl and saw that she was growing hot too; she was fidgeting around and biting her bottom lip.

Paybacc sent the girls to Domino's bedroom and put the python back in its aquarium.

"Damnnnn," Wacko said, catching a glimpse of Traquila's butt-cheeks that peeked slightly out from underneath her leather snake skin skirt. "Yo, Paybacc, you think you may need some help with that?"

"Nah, I got it faded." Paybacc smiled.

"Handle yours, cuz." Domino told his big homie.

"Oh, you know I will." Paybacc replied, giving him a pound.

As soon as Paybacc entered the bedroom and closed the door behind him, he found the girls as naked as the day they were born. Before he knew it they were pouncing on him. Traquila dropped to her knees and hurriedly unbuckled his jeans. Once his jeans dropped around his ankles, she pulled his boxer-briefs down and grabbed his tool. She stroked it up and down until it grew to its full potential in her manicured hand, right before her eyes. Licking her burgundy lip stick lips, she brought her warm, slopping mouth over his meat until she met his pubic hairs, performing a deep throat. Her eyes ran with tears and she gagged, slurping him up like he was melting. His strong hand was gripping the back of her neck and he was biting down on his bottom lip, his eyes watching her performance attentively. Slowly, she pulled her head back revealing swollen meat, inch by inch. She then smiled up at him and licked around his dick head, before taking him back inside of her dick suckers.

You nasty lil' bitch, Paybacc threw his head back and moaned in pleasure. Once Traquila felt his member throbbing, she knew that he was about to bust so she pulled back. She made her way up his marred abs, planting gentle kisses up it until she met his collarbone. Stopping there, she allowed her tongue to trace it before nibbling on his neck, creating hickeys. Unexpectedly, Passion pulled Paybacc's chin to her, sucking and biting down on his bottom lip softly. She gently pulled on it and kissed him deep and heatedly. Their lips made smacking sounds as they went at it hungrily.

Paybacc pulled Traquila beside Passion and told them to kiss. The promiscuous women obliged, making out like a couple of drunken college girls. While they were locking lips, Paybacc removed a condom from his top nightstand drawer and slipped it on. He returned to where the girls were and engaged in a three way kiss, saliva sloshing inside of all of their mouths. Paybacc told Traquila to lie on the bed with her legs spread and motioned for Passion to eat her pussy, smacking her hard on her ass. Passion crawled upon the bed, brought her mouth to Traquila's southern region and began to devour her pearl as if it were a juicy peach. The chocolate vixen squirmed and moaned as her womanhood was feasted up, loving every minute of it.

Paybacc stepped behind Passion and carefully slid his grown man inside of her moist snatch. For every inch that he pushed inside of her she made a face, each one uglier than the one before. Paybacc withdrew dick and made a slower deposit of himself until he was all of the way in. Gently he worked her middle until she'd gotten adjusted to him. Seeing that she had gotten used to his girth, Paybacc pulled her head back by her burgundy twisties and fucked her like a porn star. He hammered her from the rear as if he was literally trying to fuck her to death, and she enjoyed every minute of it. Paybacc's forehead ran with sweat and his chest glistened as he pounded Passion out, his pelvis smacking up against her. Both of the girls were screaming out that they were about to cum, which was OK with him because he was about to erupt himself. After the girls had gotten their rocks off, Paybacc pulled off his rubber and blasted Passion's butt cheeks with his pearly jizz.

$$$

Paybacc was awoken the next morning by a ray of sunlight shining through an opening in the curtains on his face. His eyes flickered open and he looked around. He found Traquila to his right with a rubber hanging out of her snatch. Rubbing his eye, he looked to his left to see Passion with dried semen on her stomach. He smiled to himself thinking about the wild time he had last night. After crawling out of bed, he pulled on his boxer-briefs and threw on his robe. It was a really snug fit but it would serve its purpose.

Paybacc made his way down the hallway and into the bathroom. He went about the task of brushing his teeth, and when he went to spit into the sink he saw the scars that he'd have for the rest of his life. He let his hand smooth over the wounds and in doing so he traveled back in time to that tragic night, and an explosion of gunshots and muzzle flashes went off in his head. The experience was so real and intense that it caused him to flinch. Paybacc's hand continued the tour down his torso rediscovering keloids and indentions, as well as the long nasty scar down the middle of him, which was a result of his surgery.

Everything had happened so fast that night that he'd gotten shot that he didn't get a good I.D on the shooter. The only thing he'd remembered about him was his eyes and the half moon scar on his forehead. Word on the streets was it was Gangsta that had blasted on him, but that was just here say. He'd known Gangsta for hustling; sure his gun went off, but not like that.

Flashback

"You sure you don't want me to handle this nigga for you?" Bully asked from behind the wheel of a Toyota Corolla, which was parked several rows way from World on Wheels with its back window to the establishment.

"Nah, I got this one, Bully," Gangsta replied, spying through the rearview mirror at the entrance of World on Wheels and waiting to see Paybacc emerge. He was in a black sweatshirt and wearing brownies over his hands.

"I'm your soldier, my nigga. This is the type of shit that I'm here for." He told him. "Use me, Blood. Let me take care of this dude for you."

"I told you I got this one, homie. Besides, I gotta put in some work every now and then to let these niggaz know this paper ain't made me soft, you Griff me? There he go," He chambered a round into the head of his banger once he spotted Paybacc exit World on Wheels laughing his ass off. His hulking frame and the faint glint of the lone gold tooth in his grill gave him away. He was in a navy blue Nike sweat suit with the draw strings pulled so tight that the hoodie would hug his head. He moved at the forefront of a pack of wolves young and seasoned, but all with the willingness to kill. Paybacc slapped hands with them all before they dismantled and headed to their respective vehicles. Gangsta watched as the

mountain of muscle staggered to his Jeep like a zombie, occasionally taking swigs of a bottle of something he had concealed in a wrinkled brown paper bag. It was apparent that he was a little tipsy.

"Alright," Gangsta pulled a bandana up over the lower half of his face. "I'm on the move." He hopped out of the Toyota and closed the door back gently. He hunched over and moved in on Paybacc as he approached his Jeep, every so often taking cover behind parked cars. By the time he reached the backlights of the Jeep his target had drove to the skating ring in, Paybacc had just climbed in and shut the door. Moving alongside the vehicle, Gangsta saw his enemy about to insert the key into the ignition. Paybacc spotted a flicker of movement in his peripherals; when he turned around he locked eyes with a pair of menacing eyes and the hollowed barrel of a gun.

The first bullet shattered the driver side window and entered Paybacc's cheek. His eyes bugged and he attempted to scream, but before he got the chance a second bullet ripped through his triceps. He howled in agony and exposed his bloody teeth. He went for his burner, which was tucked snugly in between the seat and the console, but a third bullet hit him in the chest. The burner roared back to back, shredding

Paybacc's sweatshirt and igniting flames in his abs. He looked around woozily at all of the holes in him and the crimson mess on the dashboard and interior. The splatters of blood on the windshield looked like mazes as they ran down the glass. Hearing the crunching of glass as someone approached at his left, he lazily looked over and met the hollowed barrel again. This lit the fuse in him that was to be the second fight for his life. Using all the strength that he possessed in his right arm, Paybacc grabbed the hand that the shooter clutched his weapon in. He was moving it away from his face when it fired and a bullet skinned his forehead and partially split his scalp, causing it to ooze with blood. The gun blasted again, but this time Paybacc managed to steer it clear from his dome, and the bullet shattered the passenger-side window's glass.

Gangsta cracked Paybacc in his jaw twice with his freehand until he let loose of the hand that clutched his gun. He then ran back to the Toyota and Bully burned rubber from out of the parking lot, leaving tire prints in his wake. Paybacc pulled out his cell phone, he felt lightheaded as he dialed 911. He managed to give the operator his location before he blacked out.

Paybacc was said to have been clinically dead three times, on the third try the doctors were barely able to revive him. One of the doctors reasoned that he was having one hell of a fight with The Grim Reaper. The man known as Clifton Sparrows was in an all out slug fest with death, going blow for blow until eventually, he brought the scythe wielder to its knees. The doctor thought that Paybacc must have been one bad mothafucka to have fought death and won. The surgeon had pulled a total of seven slugs out of Paybacc, some of which were dangerously close to some of his arteries. When the hospital staff had first seen him rolled through the double doors of the emergency room they'd written him off after seeing so many holes in him. But what they didn't know was that Paybacc's will to live was stronger than his notion to die. He wouldn't allow himself to be pulled over into the other side without giving the cat that shot him a dose of his own medicine. He couldn't rest in peace knowing that the fool that bodied him was still out in the streets. He wasn't going to cash-out until he got his revenge.

It took three months for Paybacc to fully recover, and once he did Bloods and Crips came to understand why his old heads had christened him with his name. He turned the Low Bottoms into World War II. With lead flying and bodies dropping, cats sighed with relief when he had gotten knocked for blasting on a couple of cops. Even with him gone the streets still weren't safe, he'd groomed a few hardheads to his likeness: Nightmare, Nike, Reboc, Domino, and Supacrip were just a few of the pups that he'd made in his image.

Present

Knocks at the door pulled Paybacc from out of the night he was shot. He rinsed out his mouth and turned off the faucet. He opened the door and found Wacko with his hand down the front of his sweatpants. "Cuz, I gotta piss." He said, rubbing his eye with his other hand. Paybacc stepped aside and allowed him in before journeying back inside of his bedroom. He stood at the foot of the bed looking over a snoring Traquila and Passion.

"It's time for these bitches to checkout." He said to himself, and drew the curtain back from the over the window, allowing the sunlight to shine into the bedroom. Traquila and Passion stirred awake reacting to the sunrays like a couple of vampires. "Come on! Come on!" Paybacc clapped his hands loudly. "It's time for everybody to go home, checkout time." He handed them their clothes and shoes, hurrying them out of his home.

Paybacc returned to the bedroom and closed the door behind him. He pulled the chest out of the closet that

Nightmare had given him and unlocked it. He opened the lid and a smile broadened his face when he saw all of the Benjamin Franklins inside. He looked up from the dead presidents and saw Wacko at the door peering in at him. Annoyed, he shot to his feet, marched over to the door, and slammed it shut in his face.

Chapter Seven

Domino and Wacko were playing a game of pool at a hole in the wall dive called The Bar Fly. The place wasn't all that grand when it came to appearances, especially when compared to other establishments. But the warm welcome and conversation folks got from the bartender/ owner Nigel and his employees made the place feel like a second home.

"When are we 'pose to be laying that thing down?" Wacko asked lining up the cue ball with an orange striped ball.

"Tomorrow hopefully; I was pushing for today but he said he had something to do." Domino said, gripping a pool stick and swigging a cold one.

"Fuck he got going?" Wacko's forehead creased.

Domino shrugged and said, "Hell should I know?"

Wacko struck the cue ball, which hit the orange striped ball causing it to land into the corner pocket. After making his shot, he moved on to his next potential one.

"You got more history with cuz than I do; I was a lil' nigga when he got caged up. He barely remembers me."

"True. I've known Paybacc since I was knee high to a caterpillar." Domino admitted. "Even when he went to the pen

I was sending him kites and dropping paper on his books. That's my big homie. I love that nigga more than I love my own father. But still, there's certain shit a man likes to keep to his self, feel me?"

"That's understandable, 'cause there's some shit hidden in here that I'm taking to

the grave." Wacko tapped his temple with his finger. He took his shot and missed it. "Fuck!"

"Stand back, junior," Domino grinned and sharpened his pool stick, "and watch a pro work." With expertise he knocked every solid color ball into its respective pocket, and concluded by dropping the 8-Ball into the side pocket. "That's game." He announced, picking up the wrinkled two hundred dollar bills he and Wacko had betted. He smiled at his homeboy and took a swig of his beer.

Wacko silently cursed having hated losing for the seventh time. Domino had been hitting his pockets all night. As a youth Domino had split time between the streets and the shooting gallery. A pool shark by the name of Larry "The Sniper" Charles had taken him under his wing and taught him everything he'd known. Larry had earned the name "Sniper" for being such a sharp shooter with the polished Oakwood stick. He was a dead-shot that never missed a ball he'd gotten behind. His life had come to a tragic end when he'd laid down the hustle on some local knucklehead. He was gunned down doing what he loved most in the world, shooting pool, and it was right before a young Domino's eyes. It wasn't until Domino had come of age that he'd exact revenge on his mentor's behalf. And once he'd done the deed he was sure old Larry's soul was at rest.

"Run that back, double or nothing." Wacko dropped two bills on the pool table.

"You still aren't tired of me taking your money, huh? Bet." He dropped his wrinkled hundred dollar bills on top of Wacko's money. "Rack'em up," He took a swig of his beer.

While Wacko went about the task of racking up the pool balls, he eased in to what he'd been wanting to ask Domino all night. "Yo, so what chu think Paybacc had in that big ass chest back at Nightmare's momma's house?" Domino shrugged. "I'm thinking it had to have been something valuable, like gold...or, uh, I don't know...money." He looked up at Domino to see the expression on his face.

"What makes you think that?"

"The way he flexed when I asked him." Wacko answered. "You saw how he hopped up in front of it, with both of the bangers all out and shit. He was about ready to draw blood behind whatever he had in there."

"And?"

"A man doesn't take a defense like that unless he's got something to protect, something of value." Wacko said, watching Domino break. Domino cracked the triangle of balls and sent a few striped ones into the corner and side pockets. "Maybe we should see about getting our hands on that chest and seeing what's inside. If there's something in there worth having, we can see if we can convince Paybacc into splitting it three ways," Domino was leaned over the pool table about to take a shot, but hearing this made him pause, and look up at Wacko. "and if he's not with it then, well…whose gonna cry over a little spilt milk?"

With a roar, Domino grabbed Wacko by the front of his shirt and slammed him against the wall. His eyes were lit with small fires and his face twitched with anger. "If you're thinking about robbing Paybacc you better drop it! That man is not to be touched! He's like a father to me, understand?" he barked on the young nigga, raining spittle in his face.

"Yeah, I understand. Now get cha hands off of me!" Wacko shoved him from off of his person and smoothed out his wrinkled shirt.

Domino looked around and saw all of the patrons' eyes on them. "Fuck y'all looking at?" he asked all hostile and shit.

"What the hell's going on over here?" An older dark skinned man wearing a black vest inquired.

"Ain't shit, Nigel," Wacko assured him with a smirk. "Just two brothers having a lil' spat, but we're good now. Ain't that right, Dom?"

Nigel looked to Domino and he confirmed it with a nod.

Wacko picked up the four hundred dollars that he and Domino had bet and handed it over to Nigel. "That's all you, O.G. We're outta here. Come on, cuz." He threw his arm over his homeboy's shoulders and walked him out of the bar.

$$$

Paybacc sat in his whip staring at a picture of his nineteen year old daughter, Zora. Zora was only six years old when he'd gotten shackled down and sent on a bus up state to do his bid. During his stretch she'd written him letters and sent him pictures. Back in prison the wall beside his bunk was covered with photos of his daughter from when she was six up until she was nineteen. Every night he would lie on his side smiling and looking over the pictures that documented his daughter's journey from childhood to adulthood until he drifted off to sleep.

Going in to do his time Paybacc was sure of one thing, his baby girl would be well taken care of. Not only did he leave her mother with a healthy sum of money, but he knew that her mother and grandmother would raise her into a respectable young lady. He was later proven right when he was sent Zora's high school diploma and a copy of her acceptance letter into UCLA. Zora was attending college for a degree in Journalism. She wanted to be a writer for some of her favorite publications and news papers.

It had been thirteen long years since Paybacc held his daughter in his arms, and just as long since he'd seen her angelic face. Zora wanted to come visit her father in prison but he wasn't having it. He didn't want her to see him caged up like an animal. He promised her that they would have their reunion, but he wouldn't allow it to be with an inch of Plexiglas between them.

Paybacc's thought took him back to the night that he had lost his freedom…

Flashback

The homeboys and homegirls from the set gathered at an abandoned house to celebrate and welcome a new addition to the family. There was alcohol and every drug you could name present. Everyone was laughing, politicking, and having themselves a good old time. One of the homie's gave young Nightmare his own gun and coerced one of the girls at the function into giving him some head. Before long it was 3 A.M and the crowd had thinned out, leaving Nightmare, Nike, Reboc and Paybacc to themselves.

"Damn, Loco, take it easy on that monkey-oil." Paybacc told Nightmare who was guzzling a bottle of Olde English 800 malt liquor. He took the 40 oz from the youth and took it to the head. Bringing the bottle down, Paybacc wiped his mouth and burped.

"Shit, cuz," Reboc said, fanning the stench of his big homie's belch.

Nike laughed and took a pull of his blunt. His eyes were so low that they looked like they were closed.

Paybacc passed the 40 oz back to Nightmare and looked up to the glowing pearl that was the moon. "We're wolves, cuz," he announced, his eyes glued on the moon. "we're wolves, and the rest of these old buster ass niggaz out here are lambs." He said, howling like a wolf. His howling drew howls from his little homies and dogs sprinkled throughout the neighborhood.

Nightmare passed the 40 oz to Reboc and Nike passed his Kush to him. Nike watched as the youngling took tokes of the Kush like a pro.

"My nigga, getting down," Nike smiled and threw phantom punches at his cousin.

"My mothafucking nigga, cuz," Reboc stated, wrapping his arm around Nightmare's shoulders and taking the 40 oz to the head.

"Under the right guidance cuz will be a reputable, stalwart soldier." Nike nodded.

"Better keep lil' cuz away from you two numb skulls then." Paybacc smacked Nike across the back of his dome, causing him to drop his blunt. Nike quickly got to his feet in a fighting stance. Paybacc swung on him again and he ducked it. From there it was on, the two crips engaged in an intense slap-boxing match.

Nike was holding his own against Paybacc for a while, but with the O.G's added height and strength he began to succumb to the brutal assault of his massive open palms. Regardless, he fought on because that's how his old head had programmed him.

Before long Reboc and Nightmare had joined the fray and an all out slap-boxing, freefall broke out. The match went on until everyone was panting and laughing.

"Lil' homie got me good, cuz." Paybacc touched his lip and came away with blood. He laughed and wrapped his massive arm around Nightmare's shoulder. "You're all right with me, loco. You're going to be my protégé. We're going to call you Lil' Paybacc. By the time I get finish molding this beautiful mind of yours," he kissed the top of Nightmare's head. "You're going to be these slobs worst Nightmare."

Suddenly, Paybacc was blinded by a bright florescent light shining on his face. He held up a hand to block it and see where it was coming from.

"Shit, its five-owe, cuz." Nike announced, dropping his Kush in the grass and mashing it out.

"It's Arsenegger and Ortiz punk asses." Reboc added, sitting down the 40 oz.

"Alright, homeboys, party's over," A voice boomed from the squad car's loudspeaker. "Clear it out."

"No problem." Paybacc said with a sinister smile as his hands crept toward his back. The homies exchanges glances as they saw him pulling a Glock 19.

"Paybacc, chill out, cuz," Nike told him.

"Yeah, cuz, you tripping, that's Popo." Nike added.

"How's your day going, officers?" Paybacc asked.

"It's going fine." The voice responded to the oldest gangsta in the yard. *"Now, move your black asses before we get out and move them for ya...Cuz."*

"Relax O.G, we'll be moving along, but before we bounce I wanted to give you something." He said.

"Now, what could your gangbanging, dope slinging ass possibly have for us, Clifton?" the voice asked.

"This!" Paybacc face twisted into a mask of hatred as he opened fire with the compact handgun.

Bloc! Bloc! Bloc! Bloc!

Smoke roared from the gun with each shot that spat from it. The bullets slammed into the door of the squad car and shattered the driver-side window. A scream of excruciating pain came from the officer behind the wheel.

"Roooool! Rool! Rool! Roooool" Paybacc howled like a wolf and laughed. *"Come on, cuz!"* he yelled to his homies as he ran and hopped the fence. The homies were right behind him. They ran as fast and as hard as they could with the squad car barreling behind them down the alley.

Everyone wore grim expressions except for Paybacc, he had an evil smile. He was an adrenaline junkie who got kicks out of putting in work. This wasn't his first time busting on a cop, last year he succeeded in killing one. The way he saw it the cops were the enemy, too. They were no different from the other hoods they had beef with.

Paybacc flung the Glock over the fence into another yard. Up ahead he saw the brick wall of a homeboy's mother's backyard.

"Pie's momma's house, cuz," He announced to his homeboys. "Hit the fence."

Still in motion, he leapt up and grabbed a hold of the brick wall. He struggled to pull himself over, while the other homies climbed over with ease. Before he knew it, the squad car pulled up and out hopped Officer Arsenegger. The sandy brown haired, blue eyed Austrian was on him like stink on doo-doo. He yanked Paybacc from the brick wall by his ankle and he fell into a pile of garbage. Arsenegger took advantage of him being disoriented, and began kicking and stomping him.

Officer Ortiz hopped out of the squad car. Blood ran from his wounded arm as he approached the beating, withdrawing his nightstick. He repeatedly struck Paybacc with the metal rod while his partner put his heels to him, stomping his mothafucking ass out. Once Ortiz had grown tired, he stepped back and allowed his partner to get in on a piece of the action.

Arsenegger pulled Paybacc up to his brow by his collar; the O.G was bloody faced and bruised. "What you gotta say now, tough guy?" he asked with furrowed brows.

"Fuck you, pig!" he spat blood into his face and laughed. The nasty red glob slid down the crooked badge's brow and outlined the shape of his nose. Pissed off, he wiped the bloody goo from his face and pulled his police issued firearm from its black leather holster. He whacked the O.G upside his head and knocked him out cold, leaving him lying on a pile of black garbage bags unconscious. Paybacc wouldn't see the streets for thirteen years after that stunt he pulled. Inside he kept his legend alive bringing drama to niggaz and being a pain in the warden's side.

Present

Paybacc tucked the picture of Zora away and put a Listerine strip into his mouth. He gripped the steering wheel and breathed in and out. He was nervous and had butter flies in his stomach. He hadn't felt like this since the first night he held baby Zora in his arms. After calming down, Paybacc slid on his shades. He grabbed the flowers from off of the passenger seat and the Teddy Bear. With a confident stride he approached the house that his daughter lived in along with her mother. He was dressed in a button-down and a tie, which he wore underneath a canary yellow Polo sweater vest and sky blue jeans over his white Polo sneakers. The duds really weren't his style, but he wanted to look presentable having not seen his daughter in a decade and change. He'd smacked on some Versace cologne and had even taken the liberty of stopping off at Good Fred's on 54TH and Western Avenue to get an edge up.

Paybacc took a glance at his yellow G-shock to make sure he wasn't arriving too early. He was told by Zora's grandmother that she wouldn't make it home from work until about 5:40 PM. It was ten minutes after. His baby girl hadn't laid eyes on him in quite some time. She didn't know he was coming to see her today, and he couldn't wait to see the look on her face when she found him on her doorstep. Paybacc took a deep breath, raised his fist and knocked on the door. For a time no one answered, then he heard the locks being undone. The door pulled open and a 5'5 caramel complexioned young lady stood in full view. She wore her hair exactly like Jada Pinkett-Smith wore hers in Jason's Lyric. In fact, she kind of resembled the famous actress, except she had hazel brown eyes and a shapelier figure.

Zora was at a loss for words when she saw her father. She put her hands to her mouth as tears welled up in her eyes and rolled down her cheeks. She leapt into his massive arms and hugged him tightly, saying, "You're home. You're finally home. Is this a dream? Are you real?" she touched his face to confirm.

"No, this is not a dream, and I'm here...right now." He assured. There was a moment of silence between them and then, he said, "My baby done got big." Excited, he picked her up and spun her around, with them both laughing and giggling. "I got cha something." he handed her the flowers and Teddy Bear. She thanked him, kissed him on the cheek and took him by the hand, leading him inside of the house.

"You want something to drink?" Zora asked her father as she placed her flowers in a crystal vase of water.

"I'll take a beer if you got one." Paybacc answered.

"Is a Heineken fine?"

"Sure. This is a nice place." He commented on the décor of the house.

"Thanks. You want the grand tour?" she handed him a beer and held one for herself.

"I want to see what your bedroom looks like."

"OK, come on." She led into her bedroom.

The colors of Zora's bedroom were pink and white. Its theme was Hello Kitty. There was a "40 inch flat-screen mounted on the wall, a chest at the foot of her full size bed, and a futon that sat against the wall. A portrait of she and her father sat on the nightstand, amongst other portraits of him in prison attire that he'd sent her. Paybacc picked up the portrait of her and him, wishing he could go back to that time before sitting it back down.

"Nice," he said of the bedroom, looking around. "You decorated it yourself?"

"Yep," Zora sat down and took a swig of her beer. "there's a lil' girl trapped in this eighteen year old woman's body." She smiled and revealed her perfectly white teeth.

"Where's your mother?"

"Oh, she's at work." she told him. "She won't be back till about nine tonight."

"How has she been?"

"She's been OK; she's supposed to be getting married to her boyfriend in March." She informed him. "You remember Wendell; the real estate broker from Flint? I wrote you about him."

"Yeah, I remember now. He's treating you alright, right?" Paybacc asked seriously, because if he found out homeboy was mistreating his daughter he was going to kill him and bury him in one of the backyard's of one of the houses he sells.

"No. Wendell's a pretty great guy." She assured him. "He treats me and mommy good, so no worries there." She patted his leg.

"Roll up."

"What?"

"Put something in the air," he pretended to smoke a blunt. "I know you smoke."

"How do you figure?"

"Cause your lips are black, and I can smell traces of it in here." Paybacc smiled. "Next time burn incents; air-freshener just masks the odor."

"Very good Detective Sparrows." She grinned and pulled her tray of weed and rolling papers from under her bed. Going about the task of rolling the blunt, Zora watched as her father leaned over to sit his bottle of beer on the dresser. In doing so his sweater vest rose up, and she caught a glimpse of the black banger stashed on his waistline.

"Still about that life, I see."

Instantly, Paybacc knew she was referring to the heat tucked on his waistline. "It's the only life I know. I just hope my baby girl isn't about to give me a lecture like how her mother used to." He made a questioning face as he raised an eyebrow.

"No. it's your life, so you live it how you see fit." She said. "But I do wanna get the chance to spend some time with you before the streets claim you."

"Don't worry, the streets won't come to claim me, and this is my insurance that she won't." he patted the heater on his waistline.

Zora put fire to the end of the blunt. She took a few puffs and passed it to her father. She watched him take a few pulls before blowing smoke from his nose and mouth.

"Oh, fuck. I forgot." Zora smacked her forehead with her palm.

"What's up?" Paybacc asked concerned, passing the blunt back.

Zora shook her head and took a few pulls from the blunt. Her eyes seemed to look from her father to something on the floor while she conversed with him. Paybacc followed her line of vision and found a blue All-Star Chuck Taylor Converse at the corner of her dresser.

"Who else is here?" Paybacc asked his daughter.

"What're you talking about? Just me and you," She looked at him crazy as she continued to get her smoke on.

Paybacc narrowed his eyes at Zora and brandished his heater from his waistline. Zora cursed herself watching her father check under the bed and behind the curtain. She jumped in front of the closet once she saw him reaching for its doorknob.

"Zora, move," Paybacc ordered with a no nonsense attitude."

"No, you just can't come in here snooping around in my bedroom and invading my privacy. I'm not a little girl anymore." She scowled.

Paybacc shot Zora a look she hadn't seen since she was a kid. She didn't know what it was about that look he used to give her, but it always shook her soul at its core. She'd heard stories about how her father gave it up in the streets. Although she didn't know if the tales were true, she sure as hell wasn't about to test his gangsta right now to find out.

Zora stepped away from the closet door, clearing a path for her father.

Paybacc pointed his heater at the door and barked, "Whosever in the closet I suggest you come out now, before this Luger tear holes in it. If you're wise you won't try my gangsta." For a time there was silence, then the doorknob slowly turned, and a dark skinned dude stepped out wearing a smile of nervousness. He was in a wife-beater and boxer-briefs, and had on one Chuck Taylor Converse. His hands were raised in surrender and quivering.

"Who in the fuck are you?" Paybacc twisted with animosity.

"Da...Da...Daniel..." he stuttered.

Paybacc looked to Zora and asked, "Who is he to you?"

"He's my boyfriend, dad!" her eyes pleaded with her father not to kill her man.

"Is this true? Are you dating my daughter?" he asked Daniel. He nodded yes.

A smile emerged on the O.G's face. "Well, that makes you practically family. Come here, bring it in." he tucked his heater on his waistline and opened his arms for a hug. Daniel looked to Zora to see what she could make of it and she shrugged. Hesitantly, the young man embraced his girlfriend's father. For the next four hours, the threesome laughed, talked and smoked weed. Daniel loosened up and became comfortable around his lady's old man. Paybacc seemed to be a laid back, down to earth type of cat.

Paybacc glanced at his watch and saw that it was getting late. He told Zora that he had to be going because he had some business he had to take care of, and offered Daniel a ride back home. Daniel took him up on his offer. Having brought their goodtime to an end, Paybacc pulled a thick knot from his pocket that was secured by a rubber-band. He removed the rubber-band and counted out ten Benjamin Franklins. He held out the dead presidents toward Zora. "Here, buy yourself something nice."

"Dad, I can't." Zora said, not wanting to take money from her old man.

"Baby girl, if you don't take this money, I'm going to take it as a slap in the face." He told her.

"Thanks, daddy," Zora took the money. She hugged her father tightly and kissed him on the cheek.

"What, I don't get a hug and a kiss?" Daniel smiled. She hugged and kissed her man affectionately.

"Bye, daddy, call me when you get home." Zora waved goodbye to the two special men of her life.

"I will." Paybacc waved and hopped behind the wheel of his black-on-black 2013 Chrysler 300 with tinted windows.

It was hot as hell so he turned on the AC and inserted Nipsey Hussle's mix-tape The Marathon into the CD player. He skipped through the disc until he found the track he was looking for: I don't give a fuck. He and Daniel nodded their heads to the music as they cruised through the streets.

Paybacc looked over at the young man and saw the tattoo on his neck: Infant Bam.

"So, where are you from, homie?" Paybacc asked casually.

Daniel told him where he was from and the said, "Zora says you're from Eastside."

"O.G," Paybacc threw up his set with his freehand. "So, Bam, are you gone put fire to the other half of that blunt or what?"

Daniel took the half of blunt from behind his ear and put it into his mouth. He went to light it and Paybacc slammed his face into the dashboard, breaking his nose. Daniel cupped his nose with both hands as it leaked like a broken faucet, pelting his Dickies and sneakers.

"Fuck you do that for?" he bellowed in pain, blinking his tearing eyes. That shit hurt like a mothafucka.

Paybacc pulled over to the curb on a quiet and dark residential block. He threw his whip in park and produced his heater. He grabbed Daniel by the front of his shirt and stuck the banger into his mouth, pressing it against his inner jaw and causing his cheek to bulge on the outside. "Listen here, you bitch ass nigga," he began, eyes dancing with madness. "Zora's on the right track with her life, and I'm not gonna sit back and watch some lil' shit like you fuck it up. She deserves better than that. You hear?"

"Yeah, man, I hear you." Daniel winced. "Arghhh, fuck , my nose, man!"

"Shut up! From now on, you and she are done." Paybacc barked heatedly, raining spittle in the youngster's face. "Don't call her, text her, tweet her, or fucking Facebook her! Because if you do, I'm gonna hunt chu down like game and split your mothafucking jugular, nigga, you understand?"

"Yeah, cuz, I got chu."

"Keep this in mind when you think you wanna get in contact with Zora…" Paybacc pulled the trigger and sent a hot bullet through his victim's cheek, creating a bloody and gaping hole. Daniel's eyes bugged and he screamed in excruciation. You could see his red skeletal jaw and teeth through the hole in his cheek. Once he'd thrown open the door, Paybacc shoved him out of the car and slammed the door shut behind him. He drove off leaving Daniel behind on the sidewalk bawling in agony.

Don't fuck with daddy's little girl.

Chapter Eight

The next day

"Did you know I sat up 'til five o'clock this morning just thinking?" Gangsta said, before he struck the golf ball. He held his hand over his brows as he watched it go up high, hit the ground, and role near the hole.

"About what?" Black Jesus asked as hid old friend as he rolled him toward the hole.

"My nephew," he answered. "What if he doesn't come outta this coma? When I first got out I felt like going at this shit hard, harder than before. But now that I think about it, maybe it's time that I take a backseat to this shit. I've been doing my thing for quite some time now, and I've made enough money to live comfortably."

"Well, if you wanna fallback, you know you have my blessing." Black Jesus assured him.

"It's not going to be easy to turn my back on this game. As disloyal and deceitful as she is, she bares some of the sweetest fruit. But this broad has a lotta baggage, man; when you think about it, do the pros outweigh the cons?"

"That depends on who you ask."

"For me it doesn't," Gangsta admitted. "It's the hardhead niggaz that don't walk away that end up getting pinched, and when they do it's for the long walk: thirty and forty years with an L. That ain't for me, Jesus. I've been behind those walls twice now. And each time was harder than the last."

"What do you plan on doing if you retire?"

"I was thinking about moving down to Miami," He confessed. "buy myself up some real estate; a few houses, a couple condos, maybe. Who knows? I'll probably open up my own business."

"Whatever you decide you have my support, my friend."

"Thanks. I appreciate that." Gangsta lined his golf club up with the golf ball. "Now back to my nephew, if he doesn't pull through there's no one of my bloodline to take up the mantle. There's Gucci, but I don't know if he's still alive. And even if he does turn up he doesn't have the head for this business. He's a hotheaded trigga-man. I love that boy to death, but he thinks there's notta problem his twin Berettas can't settle."

"Then let it die." Black Jesus stated. "When you walk away, let that be the end of it."

"I was thinking about that, but then someone came to mind."

"Who might that be?"

"Killa Dre, young nigga." Gangsta told him. "He's been holding things down in Booby's absence. He's a deadly combination; picture Gucci with the mind of Booby." Black Jesus whistled at the thought. "You're feeling me now, huh?"

"So what do you have in mind?"

"If Booby doesn't make it, then I'll pick up where he left off. While I'm running the show I'll be grooming the youngin' for that day." He tapped the golf ball. The ball rolled and dropped into the hole. "That's game." He smiled.

That night

"Can I get chu guys anything else?" Vayda asked the Muslims sitting at her kitchen table as she refilled a glass of ice water. The Muslims were hunched over their plates of veggie burgers and fries, pigging out. Their suits' jackets were hanging on the back of their chairs. Vayda had invited them in for a home cooked meal. She figured it was the least she could do. Although they were being paid handsomely for their services of protection, she wanted to do a little something extra to show her appreciation.

"Oh no, sista, everything's fine, and the meal is delicious." A Muslim wearing glasses and a red bowtie told her.

"Alright, well, if there's anything else, feel free to help yourself." She told them. "If you'll excuse me I'm going to take a bath."

When Vayda walked off the men went back to eating and talking amongst themselves.

Vayda drew herself a bubble bath and lit the lavender scented candles that surrounded the bathtub. She turned off the light, disrobed and climbed into the tub. Lying back, she closed her eyes and softly moaned, the hot water felt good on her body. She'd just about drifted off to sleep when she heard a metallic...

Click!

Startled, she sat up in the bathtub and looked to where the sound came. She saw a pair of blue Hush Puppies at the floor of the commode. Her eyes traveled up and met the flame of a Zippo-lighter, which was lighting a blunt. It was from the ember glow of the flame that she made out his face. It was Buddy, her ex pimp. Vayda's eyes bulged and she trembled uncontrollably. She wanted to scream, but she was too terrified to do so.

"What's cracking, Red?" Buddy asked, rising from where he was sitting on the commode. He began to pace the bathroom floor while taking pulls of his blunt, polluting the air with his hazardous smoke.

"You're…you're…supposed to be dead." She stuttered, her heart was beating faster and faster with each second that passed.

"Nah, baby, I'm alive and well." he assured her with that sexy ass smile of his that seemed to win almost any woman over. "Mothafucking pigs unloaded on me in the back of that ambulance, but it takes more than a few slugs to putta real mack down, nah mean?"

"But I shot chu like five or six times." She held her hand over her heart and swallowed the ball of nervousness that had formed in her throat. With that said, he stepped forth. He was wearing the same blue silk shirt he'd been wearing when she'd shot his ass. It was stained brown from his bleeding and covered in holes. Vayda's mouth quaked with terror and her stomach twisted in knots. "Oh Lord, Jesus," she cowered in the corner of the bathtub in fear for her life and the one growing inside of her.

"It's like I told you when I first gave you a taste of this pimping, baby girl," he said picking up a flying guillotine. "Once mine always mine…" He hurled the flying guillotine at her and it latched onto her head, locking into place with its spikes stabbed into her neck. She struggled to remove the Chinese decapitator, but her efforts were useless. With a grunt and a hard yank of the chain attachment, Nightmare pulled Vayda's head clean from her shoulders. The guillotine crashed into the medicine cabinet and cracked the glass into a cobweb. Through the eyes of her severed head, Vayda saw her headless body fall slump into the bathtub. Buddy laughed fiendishly with his hands over his stomach.

"Rahhhhhhhhhhh," Vayda screamed so loud in fright that her uvula shook. Her voice carried all of the way into the kitchen alerting the Muslims. The brothers scrambled out of their seats and grabbed their guns. They ran down the hallway with glasses leading the way. Damu was at the bathroom door clawing and barking at it, trying to get his way in to protect Vayda. Glasses moved Damu aside. He stood back and kicked the bathroom door at the lock, with all of his might. The bathroom door flew open, sending a spray of splinters everywhere. When glasses and his men spilled into the bathroom, Vayda was still screaming and swinging. Glasses tucked his gun at his back and shook her, trying to wake her up.

"Miss Vayda! Miss Vayda!" he called out her name over and over again. Vayda's eyes popped open and she looked around as if she didn't know where she was. "You're alright; you're just having a nightmare. OK?"

Vayda nodded and glasses wrapped her in her bathrobe. He helped her out of the bathtub and ushered her into her bedroom. She sat down on the bed. He grabbed the doorknob and made to leave when her calling his name stopped him. He looked over his shoulder at her.

"Brother Nasheed, do you mind staying in my room and watching over me tonight?" Vayda asked with pleading eyes.

"Sure. Just gimmie a sec, I'll be right back." Nasheed closed the door behind him.

Vayda looked down at her thigh and saw the tattoo she'd gotten of her ex pimp's name. She'd been using makeup to cover it up for as long as she'd been with Pavielle. She was going to get laser surgery to have it removed but changed her mind once she found out how painful the procedure was. Just sitting their staring at his name made Buddy's face pop up in her head. She imagined him laughing at her and all of the nasty things he'd manipulated her into doing. She hated any and everything that reminded her of him. Suddenly, she shot to her feet and grabbed the hairbrush from off the nightstand. Next, she took out one of Pavielle's belts from his dresser drawer and bit down on it hard. Sitting down, she scrubbed at the name tattooed on her thigh. Tears welled up in her eyes and spilled down her cheeks as she scrubbed, tearing her skin and bloodying her hairbrush. Once she'd stopped there were pieces of bloody skin stuck in her hairbrush. She dropped the hairbrush and took the belt from her mouth. She lay across the bed and sobbed her heart out into a pillow.

Sometimes time doesn't heal all wounds.

Chapter Nine

Creeper stood before a mural dedicated to his brother Puppet with a blood red candle, which sat inside of a glass that had a picture of a crucified Jesus Christ on it. He rubbed his sobbing mother's back with his freehand and watched as she kissed a portrait of Puppet and sat it in the middle of the already burning candles, flowers and cards. She then removed the rosary from around her neck, kissed it, and hung it over the portrait.

Creeper lit his candle and placed it alongside the others. He whipped out a .32 pistol and placed it beside the portrait of his brother. "For you, baby brother, just in case you run into a couple of knuckleheads up there." Creeper kissed two of his fingers and placed them against the portrait of Puppet. He then stood erect and wrapped his arms around his mother. Tears slid down her copper brown cheeks as she and her oldest son looked at Puppet's mural.

"Take care of him father; he's in your hands now." Carlita said to God of her youngest son.

The night Creeper left the hospital with Bullet and Black Jesus they went straight over to an acquaintance's house who happened to be a detective. He was one of the moles that Black Jesus had planted inside of Newton Division police department. The detective brought out the files of the two detectives that had pulled Puppet and Mira over. The files had both Detectives Ortiz and Arsenegger's personal information. Creeper took the files home and looked through them. Inside he found some very important information, like all the addresses Arsenegger and Ortiz had lived under, as well as those of their parents.

The next night Creeper stalked Arsenegger and his wife to an AMC movie theater out in the city of Torrance. It was across the street from the Del Amo mall, but next door to Lucky Strikes. He played the background watching as the married couple strolled up to the ticket booth hand in hand. They purchased a ticket to see The Dark Knight Rises and made their way inside. They bought two medium Cokes and a big bucket of popcorn to share. Creeper made sure to keep a safe distance from them so that he wouldn't get made. But even if he did happen to brush shoulders with Arsenegger he knew he wouldn't notice him under his disguise. Creeper had taken the precaution of making himself up as an old Caucasian man. He applied cosmetics to make his skin white, slid on a fat-suit, put in blue contacts, and threw on a brown, graying wig and bushy mustache.

Arsenegger and his wife entered the theater and sat in the middle row. Creeper sat six rows behind them tucked snuggly between two people in the partially crowded theater. From where he sat, Creeper watched Arsenegger and his wife behave like a couple of high school kids. They couldn't keep their hands off of each other. They were kissing, hugging, rubbing and touching. At one point during the movie he saw the crooked detective finger banging his wife. The theater was dark, but thanks to the glow of the silver screen, Creeper could make out their silhouettes. He wasn't for sure at first, but Arsenegger's shoulder movements and his wife's squirming gave them away.

Creeper was able to pull his .22 pistol from inside his windbreaker and screw on the silencer at the end of its barrel. He was going to stroll right upon homeboy and spill his thoughts into his wife's lap. Right when he was about to make his move, Arsenegger got up from his seat and made his way down the aisle. Creeper waited a few moments before following him out of the theater. Coming down the corridor and bending the hall, Creeper caught the men's rest room door closing as the dirty mothafucka walked in. He slowed his stroll and cautiously entered the men's rest room.

Creeper locked the men's rest room door behind him. He got down on his knees and looked under all of the stall doors until he saw the one his prey was in. He whipped out his pistol and entered the stall next to the one his intended kill was occupying, gently closing the door to. He quietly stepped upon the commode and poked his head over into the neighboring stall. He found Arsenegger taking a shit while whistling a tune and drawing graffiti on the stall wall. He was none the wiser to the predator looming over his head like a cloud. Creeper eased his silenced pistol over the wall of the stall Arsenegger was in and lined the barrel up with the top of his skull. He'd just applied pressure to the trigger when a cell phone rang and startled him. With that noise disturbing his action, he brought his weapon back over the wall and hunched over on the commode, listening to the detective's conversation.

"Hey, princess," Arsenegger said to his young daughter. The way he was beaming you'd have never thought he was as wicked as he was. "Yes, we're still at the theater, but we should be leaving in a minute. The movie is almost over…" he glanced at his watch.

Creeper listened as Arsenegger talked to his daughter; the more he listened the more the urge to kill him faded. His eaves dropping brought him back to a time when his father was alive. Creeper and his old man had a very close nit relationship; they were best friends as well as father and son. Marquez Santos was Creeper's hero. And when he was murdered his world shattered into a billion pieces. Creeper's father was ripped out of his life at the tender age of twelve. The tragedy left his heart bleeding and he knew it would never mend. He knew at that moment that he couldn't just murder Arsenegger in cold blood without evidence. The man had a family, and if Creeper was to rock him to sleep it would devastate not only his wife, but his little girl, a little girl that would feel the same hurt Creeper felt when his own father had been murdered. And to him that wouldn't be fair if it wasn't warranted.

Creeper wasn't a hundred percent sure that Arsenegger had murdered his little brother, but he had his suspicions. But his suspicions weren't enough for him to go ahead and sentence a possibly innocent man to death. He needed concrete proof before he performed his execution. He couldn't jump the gun and just blow the man away even if he was a scumbag. He knew that Arsenegger's name was synonymous with murders, but he wasn't on trial for those murders…he was on trial for the one that mattered the most to him…Puppet's.

Creeper tucked his pistol away, crept out of the men's restroom and through the exit doors of AMC theater. He strolled over to his rental, hopped in and drove off. Detective Arsenegger could keep his life, at least for the time being, for now Creeper was going to go digging for hard evidence, and if his suspicions were proven true he was going to be the detective's judge, juror and executioner.

$$$

Creeper entered through the doors of an Italian restaurant called Silvio's. He scanned the establishment until he spotted Black Jesus sitting in the back inside a black booth surrounded by men wearing black suits and skinny ties. They looked like they belonged in the Secret Service. Before Creeper had gotten five feet from the South American drug lord he was stopped by one of the black suits. The black suit made to frisk Creeper but he stopped him.

"Save yourself the trouble. I'm holding," Creeper raised his gold and brown Versace shirt and exposed the banger on his waistline. Seeing this, the black suit looked to Black Jesus who was in the middle of his meal. The drug lord gave a nod, and Creeper was free to join him at his table.

"I couldn't do it." Creeper began. "I was so close to the cock sucka that I could smell what he ate for lunch, and I couldn't do it. Son of a bitch has a family. His lil' girl called him right when I was finna do him, and I let'em walk."

"Why?" Black Jesus asked taking a bite of ziti.

"I can't cancel him without knowing for sure that he murdered my brother."

"Ryan Arsenegger is the filthiest vermin to have ever worked for the LAPD." Black Jesus assured him. "If you think he murdered your brother than chances are he did. If you can't bring yourself to put him outta his misery, then allow me to make a call. I could have him done away with within the…"

"No! No!" Creeper blurted, cutting him short. "I can handle this. I just need to be sure of what I'm doing. I need some sort of proof."

Black Jesus wiped his mouth and said, "My dear friend, how do you plan to get this…proof?"

"I don't know, but there's someone out there that knows something."

$$$

"Look at me doing my thug thizzle with the black dress socks on. I'd just gotten back from church and this freak bitch wanted to get it popping." Porno said, taking a sip from his plastic red cup of beer. He was giving commentary on his latest sexual romp, which played out on the "60 inch flat-screen before his mixed audience of college homies. His sex partner was a slim, pale skinned white girl with long dark hair and a teardrop ass. He had a lock on her hair and was punishing her from the back doggystyle. Porno was a USC film student who'd earned his name from his collection of amateur sex-tapes. Being a film student there was no where he went without his video camera. It was as if it were surgically attached to his hand.

"Dude, that's Naomi. I sit behind her in my Human Anatomy class." One white dude said.

"Oh, snap, that is here." a black dude spoke with his fist to his mouth.

"Shhhh," Porno hushed them, leveling his hand. "Here comes the money shot."

All of the guys said, "Ohhhh," in unison when Porno pulled out of the white girl and drenched her face with his jizz. They cheered his name, as he talked shit and slapped hands with them.

"That's right; Brian Pumper ain't got shit on me." Porno claimed, feeling like the mothafucking man.

"Yo, what the fuck is this?" the black dude pointed to the screen.

Porno turned around to see a white detective shoot a Mexican in handcuffs down in the street, and then proceed to shoot down an unarmed Mexican girl. The fellas wore shocked expressions having viewed the footage. They rewound and watched it about seven times before Porno finally decided he was sick of seeing it.

"Where'd you get this from?" someone asked.

"I filmed it while I was visiting my aunt sometime back." Porno admitted. Suddenly, the high he'd gotten from everyone seeing him in action had faded and he was now wearing a more serious look across his face.

"You've gotta take this to the police, man." Someone else said.

"I'm not taking the police shit." Porno stated firmly. "This doesn't have shit to do with me. I'ma mind my business and continue to do me. I can't speak for the rest of y'all, but I'm notta snitch."

"Porno, I really think you should take this to the cops. It's the right thing to do." the white dude urged him.

"Look, I'm done talking about this, are y'all tryna get it poping with some bitches or what?" Porno asked, brushing off the discussion. The audience erupted into cheers. The fellas were looking to fuck something that night, so what they had just viewed was put to the back of their minds. "Well, alight then." He hopped upon the kitchen counter and took his cell phone off his hip. He looked through his contacts for some women to call over.

Pussy was a beautiful thing.

Chapter Ten

Vayda stood in the doorway of Pavielle's room staring at him lying in bed. For a moment she listened to the opera that was the medical machinery he was hooked up to. Her eyes welled up with tears and her bottom lip quivered. She began to sob but quickly pulled herself together. Afterwards, she took some tissue from her handbag and dabbed her tearing eyes. This was no time to be weak; she had to be strong for her man. She knew that through these trying times he would need her the most in his corner.

Vayda approached Pavielle's bedside pulling up a chair to sit down. Taking a seat, she took his hand and placed it into her own. Her greenish blue eyes absorbed his appearance. New growth had begun to push his cornrows up from their roots, and his five o'clock shadow had reemerged. Not to mention, his lips were dry, cracked and ashy.

"Hey, babe, it's me, Vay, your rib." she informed the love of her live, grinning. "Your uncle brought me up here to see you. Well, he, Brother Nasheed and his men. They've been adamant about not letting me go anywhere alone. They take their jobs very serious, and I know that's how you'd want it. Especially with me being with our child and all..." Caressing his hand she felt how dry it was. "Baby, your hand feels like sandpaper, let me put some lotion on you." She took a bottle of vanilla scented Victoria Secret body lotion from her handbag. She squeezed some into her palm, rubber her hands together and applied it to Pavielle's hand, rubbing it up his arm. She continued to talk to him as she went about the task. "Speaking of baby names, I've been brain storming. I remember how you said you didn't want a junior because you wanted him to be different from you, and not follow your footsteps. Well, I'm teetering on Noah. Seeing how he was the one God had chosen to help him bring forth a new world. Naming him Noah could signify a new beginning. This baby could be a rebirth for both of us, our shot at redemption. A way we could start things all over. What do you think?" Not waiting for a response she continued. "Well, it's not set in stone; I figured I'd probably just wait until you wake up." She stopped applying the lotion and lowered her head. Tears fell from her eyes and droplets rained on his arm. Vayda wiped her eyes with a curled finger and looked up at her love. "I need you to come outta this coma. I need you, our baby needs you. I can't even begin to imagine a life without you. My heart crumbles at just the thought of it. So you gotta fight this shit, boo. You gotta pull through for us, and for our family. If you can't do it for yourself or for me…then do it for our son." She kissed fiancé's hand and left a lip-gloss print behind. She then rubbed her cheek against his hand lovingly. "I love you, Pavielle." Feeling a strong hand grasp her shoulder, Vayda looked over it and found Gangsta. "Oh, do you want a minute with him?"

"Yeah, the lil' punk ass guarding the door says only one person can be in here at a time." He told her.

"Alright," she rose to her feet, leaned over, and kissed Pavielle on the forehead before leaving him with his uncle.

Hands in his slacks, Gangsta stood over Pavielle's bed observing him. He looked to be so at peace in his slumber. It was as if after all of the madness he'd been through, he'd finally been granted the freedom to rest. For a moment Gangsta envied him, he'd been through a lot as well. And he was sure that there were more adversities ahead, especially with the lifestyle he chose. He wondered if death was the only way he could find his peace. He wondered if death was the only way he could escape the beautiful nightmare that was his life. He wondered, and if it somehow turned out to be true, he would embrace it with open arms.

"What's up, Booby? This is your uncle, Charles." Gangsta began. "I beat my case, and been out on these streets for a time now. I meant to come up here sooner, but I had a lot of business that needed to be taken care of. I'm sure I don't have to tell you that though, you've walked in these shoes. These Italian leathers aren't easy to fill, huh?" He said, referring to his Fennix horn-back crocodile shoes with the eyes. He walked over to the window and peered through the curtain and out into the streets below. The night was alive with the sounds of traffic, stoplights, and people moving about as they pleased. "I'm sorry, Booby. I truly am. It's my fault that you're laid up in here like this and fighting for your life. I should have been a better uncle; a better surrogate father to you and Gucci. I promised your mother and father that if anything were to ever happen to them that I would take care of you two. I promised thinking nothing would happen to them, but it did and it turned my world upside down. I knew it wasn't going to be easy raising two kids, even with the help of my mother. But I loved the two of you so much, man, that I said fuck it, and grabbed the bull by the horns." He pretended to be wrestling a wild bull by its horns. "It's the man's job to provide and take care of his family. And I failed you both miserably." His voice cracked under emotion and he looked to Pavielle with tears cascading down his face. He approached his bed, getting down on his knees and taking his hand. "I should have packed up all of our shit and moved us out to the suburbs somewhere. If I would have momma would still be alive, and Gucci wouldn't have fallen off the face of the earth, and you wouldn't be in this predicament." He put his head to his nephew's hand and cried silently, his shoulders shuddering. He had never been one to cry and show such emotions, but his family was his weakness. His love ones were his Achilles tendon, so when something happened to them it brought him down to his knees.

For a time all that could be heard inside of the room were the sounds of the medical machinery and the cries of Gangsta. Unbeknownst to him his nephew's right-hand twitched.

Meanwhile

"If I were you I wouldn't fool around with that thing. You keep toying with it and you'll trigger the mechanism that fires a bullet right through your heart. You'll be dead before your body even hits the floor." Shelly warned Gouch as he kneeled beside the cage he was inside. The cage was fixed with news papers at the bottom of it and two dog bowls. The first bowl was filled with water while the second was filled with something that resembled oatmeal. Gouch looked like a man gone mad with his nappy beaded hair and an unkempt beard. His feet were bare and his only clothing was a pair of tattered blue jeans.

Gouch was fitted with a vest that resembled a jetpack. In the back of it there were two tubes that were fixed with a green and blue fluid. The vest was fitted with three lethal fixtures. The first, once activated, was a bullet through the heart. The second was a poison that would run through the IV in Gouch's arm and kill him within five seconds. And the third was an explosive that could blow his black ass smithereens.

"You like that lil' gizmo? It's one of my greatest inventions yet. I like to call it, Death Trap." Shelly smiled and revealed his graying, rotten teeth. "I wasn't always a bum, ya know? I used to be an engineer. That's how I was able to develop lil' goodies like that baby there." He pointed to the Death Trap his prisoner wore as if it were the latest fashion. "Yeah, those were the good old days; the dough was rolling in and the women were begging to blow me. Life was great. That is until my bitch of a wife divorced me, and took me for everything I was worth. I fell into a deep, dark depression and started using heroine to cope. The next thing I know I'm living under a cardboard box." He shook his head in shamefully. He couldn't believe how far he'd fallen from grace. "Boy, I'll tell ya, life will fuck you in the ass, and won't have the decency give you a reach around."

Gouch stared Shelly in his eyes and sneered, baring his plaque teeth. Then suddenly, with a roar, he attacked the cage, rattling it and startling Shelly at the same time. The old man backed away from the cage laughing. His dogs looked at him with expressions of confusion.

"Let me out of here?" Gouch screamed at the top of his lungs, spittle flying from off of his lips.

"Ahhhhh, shuuut up," Shelly mimicked Buggs Bunny. He pressed a button on a small remote and the vest Gouch was wearing electrocuted him, until he was lying on his back smoking. "You aren't going anywhere, my friend, not until I get my usage outta ya, at least. See, I've done my research on you, Mr. Hood. You're a murdering, scumbag that slings poison to his own people. That's right, I know all about you and your brother's lil' drug crew, you guys have The Bottoms sewn up.

"At first, I took you for just another wise ass street punk, but then I saw you in action. Being a student myself, I was taken by surprise by your level of skill in Ninjitsu. Seeing this, I thought on how I could utilize your talents for my benefit. That's when I found out about this event that comes around once a year. It's a big underground fighting tournament coming up, and the winner gets one million dollars in cash. You're gonna be my fighter. All I need is the twenty grand entree fee and something suitable to wear for the occasion. That's where you come in. I want chu to go home and get whatever cash you have stashed and something snazzy for me to wear."

Gouch spit in Shelly's face through the cage. Using the wool scarf around his neck, the old man wiped his face. "Fuck you, old timer! I'm not doing shit!" Gouch barked on him. "Nigga, eat a bowl of steaming hot dicks!"

Shelly leaned closer to the cage and said, "Oh, you'll do as I wish, or I'll push this button here, and leave blood, guts, and chunks of your flesh all over this cage." His thumb hovered over the button that would activate the explosives in his prisoner's vest. Realizing that he didn't have a choice in the matter, Gouch hung his head submissively. "That's what I thought. Cheer up, Gregory. If you win I might give you a taste of my winnings." He removed the padlock from Gouch's cage. "You've got fifteen minutes to get back here. If you're not back here by then…Ka-boom!" he made the size of the explosion with his hands.

$$$

Gangsta lay in bed beside a chocolate stallion with long wavy hair. Her arm lay across his chest as she snored fast asleep. She'd been out for the past hour and a half having been fucked silly by the O.G shot-caller of the Rolling Twenties Bloods. Pulling off her thong, she expected to be let down sexually since Gangsta was a middle aged man. But he proved her wrong once he slithered between her thick thighs and gave her a hot beef injection that he was sure she'd tell her homegirls about.

Gangsta felt over whelmed with grief after coming back from seeing Pavielle laid up in the hospital like he was. Seeing him like that made him imagine Pavielle lying in a coffin wearing that same expression he had that night. He didn't know what he would do if he ever had to attend either one of his nephews funerals and had to see them lying down in a casket. That was the last thing he wanted to experience, especially after losing his sister, his father, and then later on his mother.

He never even got the chance to tell his mother goodbye because the punk ass warden wouldn't give him a pardon to leave for her funeral. He knew that she knew that he loved her dearly, and that if he could he would trade places with her at the drop of a hat. That was somewhat comforting to him, but nothing would make him feel better more than getting to see her face one last time and kissing her goodbye. The moment in time was stolen from him and he could never get it back. Just the thought of it made him glassy eyed and depressed.

Gangsta picked the fuck buddy's arm up from his chest and sat it beside her. He sat up in bed and brought his hands down his face. He looked to the dresser and saw the crack rocks the young lady had brought over. She was a stripper that did porn on the side, along with any drugs that could get her through her nightlife. She dibbed and dabbled in cocaine, ecstasy, and alcohol, but they all paled in comparison when put alongside crack. She liked to smoke her crack in a joint of weed. Cali niggas called the combination Premo joints.

Gangsta remembered Premo joints and PCP cigarettes from back in the day. Some of the homies used to get high off of them because it gave them that edge they needed to put in work. Gangsta never fucked with either of the drugs though, especially the PCP cigarettes. He'd heard a story about a friend of his brother that got wet once and broke into an Olive Garden restaurant out in Torrance. The cat drunk a bottle of Crisco oil, ate a raw T-bone steak, and held both of his hands over the burners of a stove until he melted the skin off of them.

Gangsta needed to be somewhere besides the reality that was his life. Now weed put him in the state where he was mellow and didn't give a fuck about nothing. But the way he was feeling, he needed something stronger. He'd never smoked crack before but he sold it. He knew firsthand how those tan rocks could turn someone out quicker than a pimp. He'd seen cats take a hit and never come back from it. He reasoned that it would be different for him, because he was stronger and smarter than everyone else that had tried the narcotic.

Gangsta rolled himself up a Premo joint with the Zig-Zag papers on the dresser. He put the joint in his mouth and cupped the side of it with his hand as he lit it. He was just about to take the first pull when he heard a crash down stairs. Quickly, he threw on his boxer-briefs and shot to his feet, grabbing his chrome .45 from off of the dresser. He cocked it back and chambered a round in its head.

"What's going on?" Chocolate stallion stirred awake rubbing her eye.

"Shhhhh," Gangsta hushed her with his finger to his lips. "Someone is in my house."

"I'ma call the police," she grabbed her purse from the floor and went into it to grab her cellular.

"The fuck you are. I don't need them nosey mothafuckaz in mine." He told her. The menacing expression on his face warned her of what was to come if she defied him. "They're already up my ass, I'ma go check it out myself. You lock the door once I'm gone."

Gangsta crept out of his upstairs bedroom and the stallion did like he'd told her. As stealthy as a spy, the O.G crept down the staircase with his .45 raised to his shoulder.

$$$

Gouch hopped the fence into the backyard of his house. He crept over to the window of his bedroom, hoping that his uncle hadn't replaced the latch. He wedged his fingers underneath the window and opened it. A smile broadened his face and he climbed inside. Unable to see in the dark, he slowly crept forth toward where he thought his dresser was. He bumped into the TV stand and knocked the flat-screen over. The flat-screen hit the floor, cracking its screen and shooting sparks. Gouch pulled out the bottom drawer of his dresser, revealing stacks of money underneath. He snatched a Louis Vuitton duffle bag from out of his closet and quickly began filling it. There was about sixty grand in cash total. Once he'd placed the last stack into his duffle bag, he felt the cold steel of a gun press into the back of his neck.

"You picked the wrong house to break in tonight, mothafucka." Gangsta spoke with a balled up face and twisted lips.

Gouch froze and slowly raised his hands into the air. Suddenly, he whipped around with the duffle bag and knocked the .45 from his uncle's hand. The .45 flew across the room. Gouch kicked Gangsta in the chest and the impact sent him flipping over the TV stand and slamming onto the floor. Pissed off, Gangsta got to his feet and charged his nephew. Gouch ducked when he swung, and came up punishing his midsection. He spun around and brought his heel into his attacker's head, the force behind it sent Gangsta's dome crashing into the wall and created a hole. Gangsta yanked his head out of the wall and shook the dry wall residue from his scalp. He saw the intruder stuff some shoes into his duffle bag and grab a suit from out of the closet. He was about to attack again, but the intruder's voice stayed him.

"Unc, stop, it's me!" the intruder pleaded.

Hearing the intruder's voice caused Gangsta's eyes to light up. "Gucci?"

Gouch looked to the clock hanging on the wall; he could just barely make it out thanks to the neighbor's porch light shining in through the window. He had about five minutes to get back to Shelly before he was blown to pieces. Gouch ducked out the window and over the fence, with Gangsta calling after him.

"Shit!" Gangsta cursed, failing to get his nephew to stop and talk to him. He shut the window and picked up his .45 from the corner of the bedroom. Once he returned to his bedroom, he assured homegirl that everything was OK and picked up the Premo joint. He took the joint into the bathroom, where he dropped it into the commode and flushed it down.

Chapter Eleven

Detective Arsenegger and Ortiz sat at a table inside of a sushi bar out in West Hollywood. They threw back porcelain cups of sake as they watched the sushi chef work with his special knives, cutting and chopping up raw fish. He put on quite a show tossing his knives back and forth over his shoulders and catching them. He received Oh's and Ah's like a magician at a magic show as he demonstrated his finesse with the sharp, bladed utensils. Seeing the patrons wowed caused the sushi chef to smile and boast more of his uncanny abilities.

Plates of colorful fish were sat out in front of Arsenegger and Ortiz. The seafood looked as beautiful as it did delicious.

Detective Arsenegger pushed something under the table toward Ortiz. "Take a look under the table there, by your feet." He told his partner.

Ortiz looked between his legs and saw a black leather bag. He looked up at his right-hand man and he nodded. Ortiz put the black leather bag into his lap, unzipped it, and peered inside. It was loaded with rubber-banded stacks of money.

"That's your cut from the Mitch Dollars thing." Arsenegger informed him. Mitch Dollars was a hustler out of the Pueblos that the detectives provided a service for. Anytime Mitch bumped heads with some competition, the detectives would plant homicides charges on them to get them locked up. This saved the hustler money and manpower it took to go to war. The detectives' arrangement with Mitch was a sweet and profitable one.

Ortiz smiled, zipped the bag back up and sat it between his sneakers. "So, how's Tonai doing?" he asked about his partner's little girl.

"She's doing a little better now, she had the flu."

"Man, I'm sorry to hear that." Ortiz sympathized. "Be sure to tell her that Uncle Pablo hopes that she feels better, and I'll have Cassie call her today. She's been asking about her."

"Tonai would love that." Arsenegger smirked. He took a bite of fish and wiped his mouth with the cloth napkin hanging out of his collar. "You know we were in the same hospital as you know who? Boy, what I wouldn't give to walk right up there into that black bastard's room and suffocate him with a pillow. And I would too, if there wasn't always someone watching the door."

"Maybe he'll save you the hassle of killing him and die in that coma."

"Yeah, maybe," Arsenegger wasn't counting on that happening. "I'll tell you one thing though, I'm not gonna sit back and wait to see if he's gonna checkout. I'm gonna take the incentive to make sure he doesn't come outta that coma."

The two crooked detectives clinked their drinks together and drunk them down. Afterwards, Ortiz went on to refill them. Arsenegger took a sip of his beverage, and his partner was about to indulge in his until he saw some familiar faces emerging through the entrance.

"Well, looky here," Ortiz said, staring over his right-hand man's shoulder. Arsenegger threw his head back like What's up? And Ortiz nodded across the room. Arsenegger wiped his mouth and turned around in his chair. He saw Black Jesus across the way blowing out the candles in a triple layer birthday cake.

"Why don't we go over and say hello?" Arsenegger pulled the cloth napkin from his collar and dropped it on the table. He and Ortiz moved to greet some old buddies of theirs.

$$$

Black Jesus, Creeper and Bullet sat at a table together. Black Jesus' bodyguards sat at a table next to theirs, incognito.

The patrons would be none the wiser to the bodyguards, but if someone wanted to get stupid they'd be in for a big surprise.

"Why aren't you eating, little brother?" Black Jesus asked his brother.

"I fucking hate fish." Bullet replied.

"Here, try some." Black Jesus picked up a piece of fish with his chopsticks. He made helicopter noises as he moved the fish around in the air. He brought the fish near his sibling's lips and he pushed his hand aside. "Suit yourself." Black Jesus gobbled the fish down. He looked to Creeper and saw that he wasn't eating either. "What about you? You don't eat fish, either?"

"No. Not raw." Creeper smirked.

"That's not what I heard, homie." Bullet licked his tongue at Creeper accusing him of eating pussy. His homeboy grinned and gave him the middle finger. He laughed.

"Sorry, I'm late." Gangsta approached the table with a gift and Killa Dre by his side. Killa Dre wore a solemn face, but his eyes were shifty as he took in every man at the table. "I brought you a lil' something, something," Gangsta handed the wrapped gift to the drug lord.

"Thank you. Excuse me, where are my manners?" Black Jesus said. "Gangsta, meet Creeper, he's like a little brother to me. Creeper, meet Gangsta, he's my best friend and business associate."

Gangsta and Creeper threw their heads back like What's up? And they slapped hands.

"What's up, fool?" Bullet smiled and slapped hands with the O.G.

"What's happening?" he smiled back.

"Who's this?" Black Jesus asked about Killa Dre. His eyes studied the tattoos of the young boy's face as if they were some sort of alien hieroglyphics.

"Oh, this is the kid I was telling you about. Killa Dre." Gangsta gripped Killa Dre's shoulder.

"Happy birthday," Killa Dre told Black Jesus as he shook his hand. He then slapped hands with Creeper and Bullet.

"Well, now that we've gotten all of the pleasantries outta the way, have a seat." Black Jesus swept his hand over the two empty chairs at the table. Gangsta and Killa Dre sat down, and Gangsta ordered some sake and sushi. Killa Dre declined to eat anything. He wasn't eating shit if it wasn't fried, or at least baked. He wouldn't even eat his steaks medium rare. "About your nephew, are you sure it was him?"

"Yes, I'm sure." Gangsta told him.

"You said that he came back to the house and took money and clothes, right?" Black Jesus asked to make sure.

"That's right." He assured.

"If he took all of that, then I'd have to believe that he was getting outta dodge." Black Jesus massaged his chin. "He didn't tell you where he was going? And he took cash and clothes? Maybe he's laying low until the heat dies down from that situation you were telling me about."

"Nah," Gangsta shook his head. "me and mine are of a different breed. We don't run from nothing or no body. If Gucci has an issue he knows his uncle is gonna ride with him no matter what it may be." He pounded his fist to his heart.

"He knows the kid gone ride with'em, too." Killa Dre pounded his fist to his heart. "That's my mothafucking nigga."

"I'ma put together a few guys and have them comb through the city. He's bound to turn up." Gangsta said.

"Look, it's none of my business," Creeper added his two cents. "But if your nephew packed up and got ghost how you said he did, then maybe he doesn't want to be found."

"You're right, Creeper, this is none of your business."Gangsta and the Vato stared one another down. The hostess sat Gangsta's sake and sushi plate in front of him.

"Hey, you two relax." Black Jesus told them. "Tonight's my day, my birthday. Let's celebrate and have a good time, aye? Have a drink with me. Everyone," He sat out porcelain cups for Killa Dre, Creeper, and Bullet and poured them some of the Japanese liquor.

"Salute!" everyone said in unison and touched cups. They sat their cups down and Black Jesus refilled them.

Everyone's attention was drawn by a group of people singing Happy Birthday. The hostess came from out of the kitchen holding a triple layer lemon cake with vanilla frosting with sparklers sticking out of it. The hostess and some of the kitchen staff wore party hats and blew noisemakers. They approached Black Jesus' table with the cake still singing Happy Birthday in Japanese.

Black Jesus smiled and looked to Bullet, playfully ringing his neck. "I'm going to kill you when we get back home."

"I know," Bullet smiled. "I love you, bro."

"I love you too, little brother."

Silence fell over the sushi bar as everyone waited for Black Jesus to make a wish. The drug lord blew out the candles on the cake and everyone applauded. The hostess kissed him on the cheek and told him happy birthday before leaving with the rest of the kitchen staff.

"The big forty-six, you getting up there, homie," Gangsta told him.

"Don't remind me." Black Jesus smirked. He ripped the wrapping off of the gift and revealed a black wooden box with a polished finish. A shiny metal plate was at the center of it. Emblazed in the plate was the drug lord's name, Jesus Auturo. Black Jesus smiled when he saw this and opened the lid. The inside of the box was lined with red velvet. Six Cuban cigars and a shiny metal Zippo-lighter were wedged into the opening of the velvet. "It's beautiful, I love it." Black Jesus told Gangsta. "Thank you, my friend." He held out his hand.

Gangsta shook Black Jesus' hand saying, "Brother."

"Brother." Black Jesus agreed to them looking at one another as siblings.

"Listen there's this big underground fight competition that's coming up, some of the best street fighters are going to be competing in it. I figure me, you, and a couple of the fellas could roll through. It's on me, think of it as my second gift to you."

"All right," Black Jesus agreed to the event.

"Well, don't mind if I do." Arsenegger said, taking a hunk out of the cake. He stuffed his face with it and licked the frosting off of his fingers. "Gangsta, what's up, Blood? I didn't know you were out." Gangsta cut his eyes at him, so he turned his attention to Black Jesus. "You didn't tell me it was your B-day, homes. I would have gotten you something."

"We're trying to celebrate my brother's birthday, why don't chu take a hike, huh?" Bullet told Arsenegger.

"Why don't chu shut the fuck up, Mr. Clean?" Arsenegger frowned.

Ortiz kept his hand near his holstered gun and his eyes on the men at Black Jesus' table. Bullet and Creeper were mad dogging him and Killa Dre looked like he was a second away from popping off.

"What is it that chu want, detective?" Black Jesus asked, keeping a cool and calm head unlike his guests.

Arsenegger wiped the cake on his hand off on Black Jesus' $5,000 dollar suit. Black Jesus looked to the spot on his suit where the dirty detective had wiped his hand off at. "What I want is for you and your people to climb into some body bags and shut your eyes. Now that isn't too much to ask for, is it?" The drug lord didn't say a word, and this pissed Arsenegger off royally. "You hear me talking to you, you fucking gimp?! Huh?!" he kicked Black Jesus wheelchair causing it to rattle. Bullet leapt to his feet and Arsenegger's bitch ass punched him in his mouth, bloodying his grill. The youngster went to pull his gun and Black Jesus grabbed him by the wrist before his weapon could clear his waistline.

"No, mijo! No!" Black Jesus clenched his jaws and clutched his brother's wrist tighter.

Bullet mad dogged Arsenegger and sneered like an angry pit bull. He was ready to leave that cock sucker's brain on his shoes.

Arsenegger and Ortiz's eyes lit up as they looked around surrounded, backing up with their hands resting on the handles of the holstered guns. Black Jesus' bodyguards had their guns pointed at both of them. They had a license to carry and a right to bear arms, and more importantly, the willingness to pull a trigger.

"Are you outta your goddamn mine?!" Arsenegger barked. "We're men of the law!"

"There's a phone booth by the restrooms, why don't chu call someone that gives a flying fuck?" Gangsta said, stepping forth.

"You," Arsenegger pointed his finger. "I haven't forgotten about you. My word is bond, and your whole family is dead. I swear on my little girl."

"You touch my family and you won't have a lil' girl to speak of." Gangsta said seriously.

Arsenegger lunged at the O.G, but before he could reach him, Ortiz grabbed him by his forearm. "Come on, let's go. We've gotta audience." He nodded to the patrons in the sushi bar who were all staring at them in shock. Arsenegger calmed down and adjusted his tie before casually walking out of the establishment.

Black Jesus' bodyguards holstered their weapons. Afterwards, he dropped a few Benjamins on the table to make up for the trouble Arsenegger caused and everyone moved for the exit.

$$$

"Did you see how they pulled out on us, like we don't have the law backing us?" Arsenegger said from the passenger seat taking tokes from a cigarette.

"Yeah, mothafuckaz have gotten a lot more brazen, especially to do that in a public place." Ortiz commented.

"We should have arrested them."

"If those guys pulled out like that then they definitely had a license to carry. Besides, they were doing what they were paid to do in a hostile situation; protecting their boss."

"Fucking niggers," Arsenegger stared out of the window as he took casual pulls from his square.

"Don't worry, they'll get there's soon, realllllll soon." Ortiz swore with terrifying eyes that were fixed on the windshield.

$$$

Bullet spat blood out of the window of the moving limousine and rolled the backseat window back up. "Look at my fucking grill, man! My shit is busted!" he showed Black Jesus the inside of his lip. When Arsenegger punched him he forced his bottom lip into his teeth, piercing it.

Black Jesus examined Bullet's mouth, saying, "I'll have Kiefer come by tonight and stitch that up."

"Fuck, Jesus!" Bullet elbowed the seat repeatedly. "You should have let me dome that puto."

"In a restaurant full of people? And with a gun I'm sure is dirty? That would have been genius. " Black Jesus stated. "I told you about packing while you're with me anyway. I have guys on my payroll who are licensed to carry.

They would have held us down if anything would have occurred."

"I don't know about you, but I'm not comfortable with some fool babysitting my life." Bullet told him.

"Amen to that shit." Creeper chimed in. "He wasn't the only one holding." He patted his waistline.

Black Jesus gave Creeper the evil eye, before they'd left for the restaurant he told him he didn't have to tool up because his bodyguards would make sure they were safe. Black Jesus turned back to his little brother. "Look, from now on when you roll with me, you leave your banger at home."

"Fuck you, Jesus! You aren't my pops!" Bullet waved him off.

"What did you just say to me?"

"You heard me."

"Willie, pull this mothafucka over." Black Jesus ordered his chauffer. He removed his suit's jacket and rolled up the sleeves of his button-down. Bullet pulled off his shirt and exposed the wife-beater he wore underneath.

"Wait a minute, I know you guys aren't about to fight." Creeper frowned, looking from Black Jesus to Bullet.

"Put me in the front seat with him, Willie." Black Jesus said to the chauffer who'd just opened the backseat door.

The chauffer scooped him up into his arms and put him in the front seat with Bullet. The bodyguards hopped out of their Lincoln Town Car and approached their boss's limousine. Black Jesus assured them that everything was OK before rolling up the tinted window on the passenger side.

The limousine rocked back and forth as big brother and little brother fought inside. About fifteen minutes later the passenger side window rolled down exposing a bloody lip Black Jesus. Breathing hard, he addressed the chauffer. "Willie, put me in the backseat and let's get outta here."

When the chauffer moved to get Black Jesus out of the front seat, Bullet hopped out. His nose was bloody and he had a welt below his eye. Fighting amongst him and his brother was nothing new. Although Bullet never won, sometimes he'd fight him to a standstill.

Tough love.

$$$

Gangsta and Killa Dre sat on the roof of his house passing a bottle of Hennessy between them and staring up at the stars scattered throughout the sky. All that could be heard were the crickets in the grass and their thoughts.

"Your man Bullet is a wild boy, Blood was about to bang it out with them hommies." Killa Dre said of Arsenegger and Ortiz, who are homicide detectives. "Can't say I wouldn't have done the same, though." Gangsta looked at the young nigga like he was crazy. "Don't look at me like that. Detective or not, old boy violated that man…punched him in the mouth. Tell me it wouldn't have been justified."

"It would have been stupid." Gangsta said seriously. "Airing that D out would have guaranteed Bullet a seat in the electric chair. You wanna plug a nigga like Arsenegger? Well, it's gonna take time and preparation if you wanna get away with it."

"We may need to prep." Killa Dre said. "You heard what dude said back at the sushi joint. I think he'll go after Booby."

"I know he will." Gangsta looked back up at the stars. "The question is, when?"

Chapter Twelve

"I'm sorry to hear that, sweetheart. But to tell you the truth, I had a feeling about that dude. I didn't wanna say anything 'cause I thought you may think I was just jealous." Paybacc said to his daughter over his telephone. She was crying because Daniel hadn't returned any of her phone calls. "Nothing happened. We smoked and chopped it up on the way to his house, and that was it. Listen; there are guys out there that would worship the ground you walk on. You're smart, beautiful and funnt, you can do better, baby girl. Alright, I love you, too. Bye."

Paybacc hung up the telephone and sat up on the couch, grabbing a stack of money and dropping it into a money counting machine. The dead white men sounded like a deck of cards being shuffled as they were counted by the machine. There was a beep and a green light flashed. Paybacc removed the dead presidents, wrapped a rubber-band around them and stacked them with the rest of the loot, which sat at the other end of the table. He took a pull from his blunt, dumped the ashes into an ashtray, and grabbed another stack of money. He dropped the money into the money counting machine and took tokes of the blunt, while watching the machine count the cash. The machine sounded with a *beep* and he grabbed the money from out of it. He secured it with a rubber-band and tossed it among the rest of the stacks. He punched in some numbers into a calculator and pressed the equal sign. The dollar amount was two million dollars. Nightmare had left him two million dollars before he'd passed. He had never seen that much paper in his entire life.

Paybacc lay back on the couch in deep thought as he took pulls from his blunt. He thought about all of the ways he could invest his money and triple it. One of the ways that came to mind was the dope game. He didn't know who had the strong hold on the hood since The Three Headed Monster's heads were severed, but he didn't care. Whoever called their self running the show now would have to find another hustle if he decided he wanted in.

Knock!
Knock!
Knock!

Paybacc sat up on the couch. He removed his blunt from his mouth and picked up the Calico M950 that lay beside him on the sofa.

"Who is it?" he asked, mashing out his blunt into the ashtray.

"It's Domino."

Paybacc took a quick peep from behind the curtain and saw Domino standing at his door.

"Hold on!" he yelled back. Paybacc laid the Calico back on the couch. He set aside a hundred thousand dollars and swept the rest of the loot back into the chest. Next, he locked it and dragged it into his bedroom where he placed it into the closet. He returned to the living room with a duffle bag that he used to put the hundred racks inside. He tossed the duffle bag onto the couch and let Domino in.

"What took you so long, nigga?" Domino asked, coming through the door. "What were you in here doing? Whacking off?"

Paybacc chuckled and said, "Nah, I was tryna straighten up a lil'."

"Awww, for me?" Domino batted his eyes girly like.

"You're stupid." The mountain of muscle shook his head. "You want something to drink?"

"Nah, I'm good." Domino sat down on the couch.

"Where is that fool Wacko at?"

"I don't know, but leave that crazy nigga where ever the fuck he is."

"Why you say it like that?" he picked up the Calico and laid it in his lap once he'd sat down.

Domino shook his head and said, "Ain't about shit, cuz is just a nut is all."

"I'm glad you came through, Loco. I've been meaning to get at chu about something."

"You mind?" Domino asked of the blunt in the ashtray.

"Nah, go ahead."

"What's that?" he asked, putting fire to the end of the blunt.

"Who's running the show now that The Three Headed Monster is outta the picture?"

Domino shook his head and then blew smoke into the air. "A few of the homies, including me, are doing are own thing. There isn't a governing body though. Shit, to tell you the truth I kind of like it that way. A nigga can eat right since he don't gotta pay all them mothafucking taxes. I mean, don't get me wrong, I loved the homies and all. But with them and my baby momma, I had a nigga in every pocket."

Paybacc massaged his chin and said, "I've recently came into a lil' paper and I've been thinking about getting back out there. I can start up my own operation and bring the homies under my roof and have'em work for me. And I want chu to be my lieutenant. How about it?" he nudged him.

"Cool. I'm with it, but…" Domino trailed off and shook his head.

"But what?" Paybacc asked concerned and sat up on the couch.

"Some of the homies aren't going to feel working under you." Domino spoke truthfully. "Grinding out here by their lonesome has given them that boss mentality, and if I know my niggaz…a lot of them aren't going to be comfortable with eating from off another nigga's plate, dig me?"

"If niggaz aren't tryna work with me, then that's cool, cuz." Paybacc told him. "But anybody getting dough outside of our lil' family is going to have to pay tribute. I'ma do this shit like the mob."

"What if they aren't up for that either?"

"Then they're gone feel the steel." Paybacc held out his fist. Domino nodded and touched fists with him. "I'ma need a plug though, you got anybody in mind?"

"Yeah, I can put chu on to my dude," Domino said, holding smoke in his lungs. "His prices are decent and he isn't sitting on no bullshit either."

"Fo' real? Set that up." Paybacc told him.

"Okilla," He nodded and took a pull of his blunt.

"I got something for you." Paybacc slung the duffle bag onto his lap.

"What's this?"

"Just open it up, cuz."

Domino mashed the blunt out into the ashtray and opened up the duffle bag. Seeing all of the rubber-band stacks bunched inside made his eyes bug. "How much are we talking?"

"A hunnit thousand," Paybacc smiled. "But don't let anybody know where you got that, not even Wacko."

"Man, you don't have to worry about me telling nobody shit." Domino assured him. "Good looking out, cuz. I love you, my nigga."

"I love you too, Loco." he slapped hands with his homeboy and embraced him.

Domino snapped his fingers. "That's what I came through here for. You got any shells for a .38 special? I bought it off a smoker, but the mothafucka only has three slugs in it."

"I might, man." Paybacc rummaged through one of the boxes of his belongings he'd stacked in the corner when he moved into the apartment. "I had a box of shells for a .38

special, a .9mm Browning, and a Colt .45 before I went in, but all my shit was at mom's house. You know her spot is like a shelter with all of my uncles, aunts and cousins living there. Somebody may have stolen the mothafuckaz. Oh, here they go." he took the box of shells from out of the box and his Jefferson High School yearbook fell forth. He passed the box of shells to Domino and took the yearbook from out of the box. A smile emerged on his face as he flipped through the pages, seeing how dorky some of his homies looked back then compared to their thugged out personas now. Reaching the middle of the book, he found a picture of a husky young man. He was dressed in a football uniform and down on one knee with a hog skin underneath his arm. His mug was plastered with a scowl. Staring at his eyes, Paybacc couldn't help but to think of how familiar they were. He absentmindedly rubbed his hand down his midsection over the keloids and scars he'd inherited from being shot. He picked up a black Sharpie, pulled off the cap and spat it to the side. He took the Sharpie and drew a black bandana on the lower half of the young man's face. A light bulb came on inside of his head and a look of surprise masked his face. He frowned and dropped the yearbook.

"Fuck wrong with you?" Domino's forehead creased with lines.

"I know who did this." Paybacc lifted his wife-beater and exposed his horribly mutilated abdomen and chest. Unable to stomach the sight, Domino cringed and looked away.

"Damn, Loco. Who was it that done you up?"

"Gangsta."

Chapter Thirteen

Early the next morning

"Aye, are y'all going to that party this weekend?" Bay Bay asked his homeboys and took a tall can of Four Loco to the head. He was a brown skinned kid that rocked his hair in short dreads. He was in a white T-shirt and baggy jeans. He wore a backpack over his shoulders and tied across his chest. He and his crew were posted at the bus-stop waiting on the Metro bus that would take them to school.

"You talking about the one that bitch Rebecca throwing?" this was Bolo. He was the heaviest of the threesome and had been lifting weights for the past eight months. He wore a red bandana on top of his shaved head. It wasn't to block the sun because it really wasn't that hot out. It was more so to let niggas know what color he was flying. "You know old girl stay in the Avalon's."

"I ain't stunting them niggaz, Blood, I know where my brother keeps his .380. He showed me how to shoot the mothafucka and everything before he got locked up in The Towers. If we mob to the function I'ma bring it with us." Bay Bay said.

"Bool, let me get a waterfall." Bolo extended his hand. He took the Four Loco from Bay Bay and held it above his mouth as he poured some into his mouth. He passed it back to Bay-Bay and turned to his other homeboy. "What about chu, Lil' B? You rolling with us?"

"Yeah, Blood, I'm going." Lil' B responded from where he sat on the bus-stop bench, bouncing a basketball between his legs. He was in red basketball shorts and Air Jordan 13s. He had a wicked jump-shot and a crossover that could literally snap ankles. The coach of his basketball team had christened him B.J aka Baby Air Jordan.

To anyone on the outside looking in the trio would appear to be the hardcore gangsters they were attempting to portray, but anyone in or around the life could tell that they were on the come up. They had one foot in civilian life and one foot in the gang. They hadn't earned their officials yet, but once they were given the task that would insure their passage into gangsterdom, they were going to execute it with precision.

"Now, you know Blood going, especially since Jennifer said she's gone be there." Bay-Bay claimed with a smile. "You know that's wifey and shit."

Lil' B sucked his teeth. "Come on now, it's going to be way too many bitches up in the spot for me to be sweating, sis. I live by the Three F's motto: find'em, fuck'em and flea'em."

"So you hit that?" Bay Bay inquired.

Lil' B was hesitant on answering at first. "Yea…yeah," He stammered.

Bay Bay sucked his teeth and said, "Nigga, you're lying. It took you too long to answer."

"Fuck I gotta lie for?" he mad dogged him.

"Blood, stop lying on your dick, you know good and goddamn well you didn't hit that." Bolo chastised him.

"Alright, I'ma keep it a hunnit. I didn't fuck, but I did finger that bitch." Lil' B swore.

"When?" Bay Bay side eyed him.

"Man, fuck y'all niggaz, I don't have to prove nothing to y'all." Lil' B put in his earphones and searched his IPod until he found the song he was looking for Dr. Dre's Bang Bang. Finding it, he turned up the volume and nodded his head to the music. He looked over to his right and found Bolo and Bay Bay slap boxing. He watched them for a time, then closed his eyes and continued nodding to the music. Suddenly, Lil' B felt something warm splatter against the side of his face. He slowly opened his eyes and felt the side of his face, his fingers coming away with blood. He looked over his shoulder and saw Bolo's face twist in agony as bullets entered his front and exited out of his back. His blood decorated the graffiti scrawled wall behind him with crimson splatters. Pedestrians scrambled and ran as slugs flew, laying some down and narrowly missing others. Lil' B wanted to take off running but fear had paralyzed him from the waist down. It was like he was being weighed down with cement shoes. He looked over his other shoulder and Bay Bay was hauling ass down the street holding his arm. Looking back around, he found three men wearing hockey masks approaching him, all holding smoking weapons. The biggest and most intimidating of the men was at the middle of the trio. A slimmer man was on his left and a shorter was on his right. The bigger man motioned for the shorter man to take care of Bolo and for the slimmer man to take care of Bay Bay.

Music still playing in his ears, Lil' B watched as the shorter man approached Bolo with an AR-18 and gave his body a quick spray. He looked to the slimmer man and he'd just chased Bay Bay into the street and cut him down with his MP-5. The bigger man put his Calico to Lil' B's chin and turned him to face him. The bigger man had a pair of dark, evil eyes that seemed to peer into his eyes and look straight into his soul. He snatched the earphones from his ears and threw them aside. Lil' B trembled uncontrollably. He closed his eyes and hot tears shot down his face. The bigger man looked down and saw a stain growing in youth's basketball shorts, a pool of yellow fluid was quickly forming between his sneakers.

"Please, don't kill me, man." Lil' B said with pleading eyes as he quivered all over.

"I'm not gonna kill you, I want chu to deliver a message to Gangsta." The bigger man replied. He cocked back the hand holding the Calico and swung it back around with all of his might.

Crack!

Lil' B hit the sidewalk unconscious. The bigger man threw him over his shoulder and carried him over to a '72 Plymouth Duster. He dumped him into the trunk, slammed it closed and drove off.

That night

Lil' B's eyes were bloodshot and rimming with tears ready to roll down his already slick cheeks. He lay in bed wearing a hospital gown. He closed his eyes and tears fell. He struggled to finish telling his story, because he didn't want to relive it.

"It's alright, take your time." Monk said, gripping his son's shoulder with his one good hand. His eyes had grown glassy seeing how torn up his boy was.

"What happened after that?" Gangsta asked Lil' B. He and Killa Dre were standing beside the youth's bed across from Monk.

"The next thing I remember was waking up in front of the hospital with this." Lil' B held up his gown showing Gangsta the note carved into his torso: *I know you were the one that shot me back in '93. Paybacc is a mothafucka.* "I tried to get up but..." he closed his eyes and tried to summon the strength to finish his story.

"But what, B?" Gangsta asked concerned.

Lil' B swallowed hard and continued, "They were gone."

"What was gone?" he asked wearing a confused expression.

"My feet..." Lil' B's voice cracked with emotion. His eyes welled up with tears and his bottom lip quivered. He drew the sheet back from his legs; his feet had been hacked off at their ankles. Gangsta and Killa Dre turned away not wanting to see the grotesque sight. It twisted their stomachs and made them sad all at once. It was apparent that Lil' B's hoop dreams had been snatched from him, and he'd never introduce the world to his famous jump-shot. Lil' B buried his face into his father's chest and sobbed loud and hard. Monk rubbed his son's back trying to comfort him. Finally, the tears came spilling down his face.

"He cauterized his wounds so he wouldn't bleed to death. He wanted him alive so you could see a taste of what's to come." Monk told him, wiping his eyes with a curled finger. "Do you have any idea who this cat is?"

"Paybacc," Gangsta answered with his back to Monk. He had his hands behind his back and was staring out of the hospital window.

"Paybacc? I thought that mothafucka was locked up." Monk frowned.

"No. He's free."

Killa Dre's cell phone ranged. He answered it. "Holy shit, where at? Yeah, I'm up here with him right now. I'ma slide through there in a minute." Gangsta and Monk exchanged glances wondering what Killa Dre was talking about on the phone. The young nigga ended the call and put the cell phone back on his hip. "Yo, man, that was Bourne. He said they just found Lil' B's feet on 29th and Griffith hanging on a phone-line like some fucking sneakers." The news made Lil' B sob even harder. It got so bad that the doctor rushed in and asked them to step out, while she injected him with something that put him at ease and made him fall asleep. Gangsta, Killa Dre and Monk went into the waiting room.

"So you got at this cat back in '93? What for?" Monk asked. Gangsta nodded to Monk's stump causing him to rub on it. "He took my arm, and now he's taken my son's feet. He's got to go, and he's got to go tonight!" he said, jabbing the air with his finger. "Me and you can get this nigga, man. Me and you can ride like how we used to back in the day. I gotta 12 gauge shotgun and an Uzi I left down here at Valerie's before I shook out to The Dale." Before he'd lost his arm in a drive by shooting, The One Arm Monk, or Monk as the homies called him, was a man that was quick to violence and had solved all of his disputes from behind the trigger of a pistol. He'd been one of the top earners in Gangsta's operation, but after accumulating enough dough to live comfortably, he decided to turn his back on the game and move out to Palm Dale. He'd tried time and time again to get his son Byron .Jr, or Lil' B as he was called around the hood, to come with him but the boy insisted he stay with his mother.

He knew he hadn't always been the best father, and he wanted to remain in his son's good graces, so he let him stay in the hood with his mother. It was a decision that he'd regret for the rest of his life.

"Shhhh," Gangsta hushed Monk with a finger to his lips. He pointed at the door: there were Caucasian detectives talking with Lil' B's doctor out in the hall. The doctor nodded to something one of the detectives said then she motioned for them to follow her. "I figured they'd come snooping around sooner or later."

"Man, I can't stand them mothafuckaz." Killa Dre said to no one in particular, his right-eye twitching with hatred.

"So what's the plan, Stan? Are we gone air hole this fiddle, or what?" Monk asked eagerly.

"I just got outta the joint, Monk. I'm not in a hurry to go back." Gangsta told him.

"I can respect that." Monk said, removing his bucket hat and wiping his sweaty forehead with a handkerchief. He tucked the handkerchief into his back pocket and adjusted his hat. "I'm B.J's daddy, so I'm his keeper. My gun is gonna go off whether or not yours is there to back it." The one armed man made to leave but Gangsta stopped him by grabbing his shoulder.

"Hold on, Monk. There's no need for you to bring your gun outta retirement." He told him. "I got something else in mind."

"What's that?" A line went across Monk's forehead.

"I'ma put some change on this nigga brain," Gangsta replied, rubbing his hands together. "Fifty racks for whoever brings me Paybacc, another fifty if he's alive. Y'all hit them streets and spread the word. It's open season on this nigga."

Blood would answer for blood.

$$$

Paybacc stood at the center of the garage pounding away at the blue Everlast punching bag that hung from the ceiling. The punching bag swayed back and forth as the O.G slammed his bandaged wrapped fists into it. His face wore a coat of sweat and perspiration made his hairy chest glisten under the florescent light.

The garage door opened with a squeal, but he paid no mind to the two men at the corner of his eye. They'd have to wait until he was done. He was solely concentrating on punishing the punching bag at the moment. Paybacc threw his four last hooks to the bag, with the fourth one being the most powerful. Chest heaving, he picked up a bottle of water and a towel. He wiped his shining form down and took a swallow of water. He sat down in a chair, sat the bottle of water aside and began un-wrapping his hands.

"What's up with y'all niggaz, man?" He asked, not bothering to look up as he was un-wrapping his hands.

"We threw that lil' nigga'z feet over the phone-line on 29th and Griffith like you told us." Domino said, jabbing the punching bag.

"Did anyone see you?" Paybacc asked, looking between them both.

"Nah, no one saw us, I'm sure of it." Wacko assured. "I was keeping an eye out. If there were anyone out there I would have burnt them." He adjusted the burner on his hip.

"What about the kid?" Paybacc inquired.

"He's good, cuz, we dropped him off in front of emergency at County and we torched the car." Domino said, pulling off his black sweatshirt and continuing to thrash the punching bag.

"I don't think we should have left that fool alive." Wacko said. "What if we happen to get picked up and shoved into a lineup? He could remember some distinction about us to point us out."

"Even if he does remember something that could I.D us, Gangsta wouldn't allow him to open his mouth. He would rather keep that lil' info for himself and come hunt us down."

Wacko nodded in agreement.

"What's our next move?" Domino asked as he worked up a sweat.

"I'll keep you in the know." Paybacc said, leaving the garage.

"Aye, cuz," Wacko addressed Domino in a hushed tone. "That mothafucka is a couple of grams short of a kilo. You saw the look in that nigga'z eyes while he was sawing that lil' dude's feet off? You can't tell me he doesn't have the Devil in him."

Domino smirked as he was pummeling the punching bag. "Yeah, cuz is a lil'off kilter, but that's my big homie. Besides, that lil' dude was the enemy and you don't show mercy to your enemy."

"Still, he could have just bucked the lil' nigga down; sawing off his feet is grotesque. That's some maniac, serial killa type of shit. I'll let my gun go, but I don't have the stomach for all of the extras. Feel me?"

"You always talked about how you wanna be known as the most down and reputable young nigga from the set, right?

Well, that lil' stunt we just pulled will for certain be all over the news, and with it our names will spread throughout The Bottoms like the Bubonic Plague. You won't be famous…you'll be infamous."

Wacko nodded his head and massaged his chin as he thought on it. "I can dig it, but after we twist these faggots…I'm staying the fuck away from that psychopath."

"Chill, Paybacc ain't all that bad." Domino argued. "Hell, he dropped me a hundred racks."

"He dropped you a hundred? When?" Wacko inquired as he approached.

Domino cursed himself for his slip of the tongue. "I said he dropped me a hundred dollars."

"The fuck you did." Wacko smiled, making him look like a rodent. "You said he dropped a hundred racks on you. If he gave you a hundred racks just cause, then I know he gotta be holding a mill or better, and I bet its stashed away in that chest. I knew that mothafucka was holding a big bag. What I tell you, cuz?"

Domino wiped his face with a towel and said, "Either way, we're still not sticking him for it. Tomorrow, my young nigga," He threw the towel over Wacko's head and left the garage.

Wacko planned on snatching that money from Paybacc whether Domino agreed with it or not. The way he was on it, his ass could get a chest full right along with the O.G if he got into his feelings about it.

Chapter Fourteen

Creeper stood looking over the ledge of an apartment building fumbling with an AK-47 assault rifle. His hair was a mess, his eyes were bloodshot, and his cheeks were slick with tears. He was drunk out of his mind and emotional. He took a bottle of Tequila to the head then sat it upon the ledge. He aimed the assault rifle at a black & white police car cruising through the block below. He gently placed his index finger on the trigger and pulled it back. The choppa rattled to life in his hands and vomited sharp rounds of ammunition. The barrel of the weapon ignited with fire as empty shell casings were discharged from the side of it. Creeper laughed maniacally as bullets rained on the rooftop of the police car below, turning it into Swiss cheese.

The police car lost control and crashed into a cluster of trash cans and garbage bags. Creeper relieved the trigger once he heard his weapon click empty. He slung the smoking assault rifle aside and took the bottle of liquor to the head again. This time until it was empty and only the worm was left. The worm slid down the slick neck of the bottle and into his mouth. He crunched and swallowed it down. Afterwards, he took one last look at the bottle and tossed it to the side. The bottle hit the graveled rooftop and shattered into broken glass.

Creeper staggered toward the door of the rooftop lighting up a Newport cigarette. He took a pull and then blew smoke into the air as he disappeared into the doorway.

Since Puppet's departure into the afterlife, Creeper had been an emotional wreck. To anyone on the outside looking in he seemed to be dealing with his brother's death fairly well, but he had always been good at hiding his true feelings and emotions. It was one of the many things his father had taught him before his passing. He knew how to play his hand to his chest and show an unwavering attitude. It was a great quality to have as a boss whether your business was in the streets or in the corporate world.

Puppet had been Creeper's heart, and waking up without him felt as if he had a transplant. Puppet was gone and now there was an ice-box hidden in Creeper's left-breast. There was a coldness there that only the North Pole had experienced and it had left him with an "I don't give a fuck" attitude. He no longer cared about money, cars, clothes or bitches. Hell, he didn't even care about himself. Sometimes he wondered why he even went on living. Life had brought him many disappointments, and he was sick and tired of having to deal simply because you were looked upon as weak if you opted for a quick way out through suicide. He felt that if a person chose to take his or her own life then that was their business, and people had no right to pass judgment on them.

Creeper staggered out of the apartment building taking pulls of his Newport. Before him he saw two police cars parked counter clockwise to the police car whose rooftop he'd aired out. There were three police officers surrounding an officer that was lying in the street being attended to by another officer.

"Aye, did you just come out of this building?" An African American police officer approached Creeper pointing his gun to the white apartment building behind him. His other hand held a flashlight, which he'd been using to search the night for whoever that blasted on his partner. Creeper paid the African American officer no mind; he continued to smoke his cigarette and watch the officers before him as if they were on a movie screen. "Yo, do you hear me talking to you?" the African American officer tapped him on his shoulder with his flashlight. Creeper looked to the officer as if he was a moviegoer interrupting his movie. "Did you just come out of this building?" he pointed again to the white apartment building. Creeper looked behind him at the apartment building and then to the officer again, shaking his head no. By this time three more officers approached him.

"Did you hear anything, or see anyone?" The African American officer asked as he holstered his firearm.

"If you want me to do your job hand over your gun and badge." Creeper said smugly.

"Now isn't the time to fuck around, asshole." A Caucasian officer with red hair warned with a hard face. "One of our own has been shot, and he might lose an arm and a leg. So if I were you, I'd try to stay on our good side."

Creeper looked around at all of the faces of the officers and they were wearing scowls. A lesser man would have been fearful, but he had the heart of a lion and the balls of an elephant. No man breathing the same air as him could ever instill fear in him. He stood firmly on The Notorious B.I.G's motto Them Niggas Bleed Just like Us. Creeper took one last pull of his cigarette and flicked at the African American's polished black boot, this caused the officers to brandish their nightsticks, one by one. Creeper unzipped his pants and pulled out his meat. With an unsteady aim, he pissed all over the Caucasian officer's boot and pants leg.

"Cock sucker!" the Caucasian officer bellowed angrily and struck his disrespectful ass upside the head with the nightstick, sending him crashing to the sidewalk. The officers kicked, stomped, and pummeled Creeper with their nightsticks. The Caucasian officer motioned for the officers to give him room, leaving the Vato on his hands and knees bleeding. He spat blood onto the ground and looked up at the Caucasian officer just as he was removing his pistol from its holster. The officer pointed his weapon at the Vato's head. Creeper slowly leaned forth and wrapped his lips around the barrel of the officer's gun. The Caucasian officer looked around at the other officers with a look of confusion, his forehead wrinkled.

"Do it, release me! Please!" Creeper closed his eyes and tears rolled down his face.

"This mothafucka is crazy, man." The African American officer said. "Leave him be. I'll radio an ambulance for Brewster." He pressed the button on the radio transceiver on his shoulder and asked for an ambulance.

The Caucasian officer took his pistol from Creeper's mouth and holstered it. The officers walked off and left the Vato on his knees.

"Where are you going?" Creeper yelled. "Hey, get your lily white ass back over here! You're supposed to kill me, you fucking pussy!" Seeing that the officers weren't paying him any mind, Creeper slowly got to his feet and staggered off wincing and holding his side.

$$$

Creeper came through the door of his condo hearing the blare of the TV inside of the living room. He staggered into the living room and found his mother fast asleep with his little sister snuggled close to her. The glow of the TV shined on them as a late night infomercial played. Creeper took a blanket out of the hallway closet and draped it over his mother and sister. He leaned over and kissed his mother and sister on their foreheads. He then picked up the remote control to the flat-screen and turned off the TV.

Creeper made his way up the staircase removing articles of clothing as he went along. Once he entered his bedroom and closed the door behind him, he finished taking off his clothes and stepped into the shower. He washed himself of the dry blood and dirt that covered his form. After showering, he sat down on his bed and began drying his hair with another towel. Once he was done, he removed a Colt .45 from his drawer. He checked the magazine for a full clip, inserted it back in, and cocked it. He took a moment to himself, closing his eyes and allowing tears to coat his cheeks. He took a deep breath and put the Colt into his mouth as far as he could.

Through glassy eyes he viewed the portrait of him and his little brother when they were just kids sitting on his dresser. He closed his eyes tightly and wrapped his finger around the trigger. Just as he began to apply pressure to it, there was a knock at the door. Creeper took the Colt out of his mouth and asked, "Who is it?"

"It's Arlene, Ruben." His five year old sister replied.

"Uhhhh, hold on." Creeper said. He stashed his burner back into his dresser drawer beneath his underwear. He then threw on a wife-beater and some pajama pants. He opened the door and found the world's cutest little girl standing before him, rubbing her eye.

"Can I sleep in here with you tonight?" Arlene asked.

"I, uh, sure," Creeper said. "as long as you promise not to fart in your sleep."

"I won't, I never fart in my sleep." Arlene smiled.

"OK. Come on." Creeper grinned and drew the covers back for his little sister. Arlene hopped into the bed and pulled the covers over her person. Creeper turned out the lamp light and turned over in bed.

Arlene kissed him on the cheek and snuggled against him. "Goodnight, Ruben. I love you."

"I love you too, mija." He kissed her on the top of her head.

Lying there with his eyes closed, Creeper knew he'd never attempt to take his own life again. He had to live to find out exactly what happened on the night his brother was shot down in the streets. But most importantly, he had to be around to provide and protect his mother and little sister.

The next day

"How long have you been doing business with this cat?" Paybacc asked Domino from the passenger seat, where he stared out of the window fumbling with a toothpick at the corner of his mouth.

"A couple months now," Domino said, navigating the off white Cadillac Seville through the streets.

"You sure homie ain't a Fed?" Paybacc asked.

"Yeah, I'm sure." Domino said. "His name gotta lil' weight to it in these streets. He isn't under any paperwork either, I made sure of that. What chu think I just dive in that water without checking for sharks first? I'm smarter than that."

"I've taught you well, grasshopper." Paybacc said in a Kung Fu Master like voice and patted Domino on the shoulder. "You told'em I want ten of them thangs, right?" Domino nodded yes. "If his stuff is as good as you claim it is I plan on doing a lot more business with this cat."

"I think that's him up ahead." Domino nodded to a lone figure standing beside a car in the middle of the desert.

"You know what gets me?" Paybacc asked never taking his eyes off of the lone figure. "Why'd he choose to meet up way out here?"

"Who knows? Why don't chu ask'em yourself." Domino replied.

The Cadillac Seville pulled upon the lone figure. He turned out to be a youthful looking Mexican cat. Domino and Paybacc hopped out of the Cadillac and approached him. The expression he wore was a solemn one. The first thing Domino noticed about him was the cuts and bruises on his face.

"Damn, G, what happened to your shit?" Domino asked, slapping hands with him.

The Mexican felt his face and grinned, "I cut myself shaving."

Domino chuckled and gave Paybacc a nudge, introducing him, "Yo, this is my man Paybacc." Domino had talked with his plug a few weeks before about his man that wanted to cop some bricks. At first the plug was reluctant about doing business with someone new, but submitted since he and Domino had such a good business relationship that he didn't want to sour. New money was always good, but sometimes it came with a high price. Cats would be in a bad way, and would sacrifice some other poor bastard to avoid a Federal stretch. The plug had no plans on being one of those "poor bastards" and if he even got the idea that a dude was a rat he'd walk away without looking back.

The quote and quantity had already been negotiated by Domino, now only the exchange would have to be made. The plug chose their meeting place because there wasn't a soul in sight within miles and miles of them. They were practically in the middle of nowhere.

"What's up?" Paybacc raised his large mitt to slap hands with the plug. The plug left him hanging and he dropped his arm to his side.

The plug looked to Domino and asked, "Is this dude copasetic?"

"Yeah, cuz, my nigga A1," he assured him, "I vouch for this man."

"Are you willing to put your life on it?" The plug asked with a dead serious gaze.

"Yes." He held the plug's gaze and seriousness.

Paybacc sighed and rolled his eyes. "Look, man, I'm not wearing a wire, see." He held up his shirt and exposed his hideous scars and keloids on his torso. The plug looked to Paybacc's crotch. "All right, I see where you're going. You think a nigga gotta wire taped to his nuts." He made to unzip his jeans, and the plug held up a hand.

"That isn't necessary." The plug told him then turned around. He seemed to be looking at someone far in the distance when he gave a sign like an umpire. Domino and Paybacc narrowed their eyes trying to see who he was communicating with. Straining their eyes they made out a man two thousand yards away behind the scope of a sniper rifle lying on the rooftop of an SUV.

The plug motioned for Domino and Paybacc to follow him to the trunk of the rental he'd purchased. He opened the trunk and exposed ten White Bitches with a stamped picture of a black Jesus Christ on them. Paybacc licked his chops and rubbed his hands together greedily thinking about the dough he was about to make off of the white hoes.

"Cool?" The plug asked.

"Cool." Paybacc smiled.

"Alright, show me the fedia."

Paybacc popped the trunk of the Cadillac Seville and Wacko was stashed inside. The knucklehead smiled wickedly and racked his shotgun. The plug raised his hands and gave Domino an evil glare.

"Chill, papi, this is square biz." Paybacc assured him. "Domino was sure of you, but I don't know you like that, so I took a precaution." Wacko climbed out of the trunk and handed his big homie a duffle bag. Paybacc handed the duffle bag over to the plug and he peered inside. Satisfied, he threw the duffle bag over his shoulder.

"If this shit is as good as my boy tells me it is, suspect to be doing a lot more business with me." Paybacc told him.

"I look forward to it." The plug replied.

"I didn't catch your name, homie." Payback raised his hand.

"Creeper," The plug slapped hands with him.

Chapter Fifteen

"Man, ain't no telling when this fool gone make another stop." A stud dressed in all black said from the backseat of a white Honda Accord. A sawed-off double barrel shotgun was grasped in her meaty palm. "I told y'all we should have got out and sprayed him at the light a ways back."

"Nah, fuck that," A light skinned fellow wearing a beanie and trench coat said. "This mothafucka is only worth fifty racks stiff, and a hundred alive. I want him breathing if possible."

A slim dude in a baseball cap and shades tapped a small vial of cocaine out onto his fist and snorted. He batted his eyes and turned to Beanie with a flaring red nose, wiping it with the sleeve of his jacket. "A hundred big ones, huh? Shit, I would have sung this baby a lullaby for five grand."

"Well, let's see what chu gone do for a hundred. There he goes," Beanie said, seeing their target hop out of his car and head toward the liquor store. He turned to the backseat. "La'chat, pass me them thangs from back there." Beanie took the weapons up front as they were passed to him. He held onto the Mossberg pump while baseball cap took the M-16. Beanie cocked the slide on his weapon and baseball cap pulled back the hammer on his. "Me and this fool are going in, you keep a watch on the door in case he makes it past us. Remember try not to kill'em. He's worth more to us alive."

"I gotchu," The stud replied caressing her sawed off as if it were the hide of a horse. From the backseat window she watched her partners in crime jog across the street and into the liquor store.

It was time to get paid.

$$$

"Let me get a bottle of Patron, Cigarillos, and a box of Maggies." Paybacc said in his signature husky voice from underneath his hoodie. When the Asian clerk went to gather the items he requested, the O.G went to get a couple more things. He was looking through the glass doors of the refrigerator at the alcohol beverages when the bell chimed twice signifying two persons entering the store. Hearing this, he glanced up at the round mirror that sat high in the corner of the store. The mirror casted a broad view of everything inside of the liquor store. Paybacc saw two suspicious men enter the store: the first one wore a baseball cap and shades. The second one wore a beanie and a sweatshirt underneath a trench coat.

Something in Paybacc's head screamed for him to get the hell up from out of there, but he ignored it. He then went on to remove two .40 oz bottles of Olde English from the refrigerator and walked them toward the counter. That's when he saw the two suspicious men pretending to be looking for something as he approached the counter.

The Asian clerk gave Paybacc's the total for his items, "$58.33."

Taking a brick of money from out of his pocket, Paybacc pulled a hundred dollar bill free and placed it on the counter. Next, he glanced over his shoulder, seeing the men were still pretending to be looking for items. He turned back around and the clerk was counting out his change. Paybacc stared into the clerk's eyeglasses and saw the men making their move through his lenses, weapons at their sides. After peeping this, he snatched one of the .40 oz bottles of Olde English from the counter. Then spun around and launched it at baseball cap's head just as he was lifting his assault rifle. The bottle exploded into broken glass, drenching the man's face and knocking him off his feet. Paybacc drew his Tec-9, but Beanie was a lot quicker on the draw. Beanie walked forth discharging his Mossberg pump; the first blast tore several bags of potato chips on a rack into shreds while the second slammed the clerk into the liquor bottles behind the counter. The bottles toppled over hitting the floor and breaking into pieces. Beanie continued to blast on his mark as he ducked and ran out of the store, trying to avoid getting his mothafucking melon blown off.

"Haa! Haa! Haa! Haa!" Paybacc came running out of the liquor store, occasionally glancing over his shoulder to see if the gunmen were following him. Suddenly, a blast sent flipped him and sent him skidding down the alley.

"Got that ass," La'chat lowered her smoking sawed-off and pumped her fist victoriously. She then went jogging in the direction of her kill.

"You get'em?" Beanie asked.

"Hell yeah."

"Is he dead?"

"I don't think so. I aimed for his shoulder."

Baseball cap walked upon the twosome holding his bleeding skull and glancing at his crimson hand. "Where that nigga at?" he asked the stud, and she pointed down the dark alley. The threesome followed a sprinkled blood trail and found Paybacc at the end of it, groaning in pain. He was still alive.

"Yeah, this mothafucka still kicking; Chat, gimmie those zip-cuffs." Beanie held out his hand for what he'd asked for. The stud went to pull the zip-cuffs from her back pocket when a pair of headlights blinded her. She made to run, but it was already too late. A Chrysler 300 impaled her to a brick building, crushing the lower half of her. La'chat screamed out in excruciation and pounded the hood of the vehicle with her fists, angrily. Seeing that baseball cap and beanie were taken off guard, Paybacc took advantage of the diversion. He scrambled to his feet and recovered the stud's sawed off and the Tec-9 he'd dropped when he was shot. He whipped around with the sawed-off. It recoiled when it blasted baseball cap full in the chest, throwing him up against the wall of a neighboring building. The wounded man hit the ground on his side and fell onto his back wearing The Face of Death. Using the Tec-9, Paybacc shot beanie's legs out from under him from beneath the car.

Hearing beanie holler and collapse to the ground, Paybacc ran upon the hood of the Chrysler 300 looking to wrap up some unfinished business. Beanie was busy howling in agony, but once he saw a pair of evil eyes staring down at him he forgot all about his mangled legs. He went to raise his shotgun but it was already too late, slugs shredding up the side of his face made this apparent. Homeboy wore a mask of horror. His eyes were bugged and his mouth was a gap, blood pooling at his lips.

Paybacc lowered his Tec-9 and looked through the windshield of the Chrysler 300. Domino was behind the wheel while Passion and Traquila were stashed in the backseat wearing faces of worry. Hearing the stud bawling, brought Paybacc's attention over his shoulder where she was wedged between the Chrysler and the building. Police sirens wailed in the distance, but he didn't give a mad ass fuck. He jumped off the hood of the car and approached the stud, gripping his weapons firmly. He sat her sawed-off on the hood and pressed his Tec-9 into her bottom jaw, indenting her face.

"Who sent chu?" Paybacc scowled and gritted.

"I don't know," The stud croaked in pain.

"Bullshit!" he roared in her face, spittle flying.

"No!" she shook her head fast. "There's a bounty on you."

"How much?"

"Paybacc we need to get the fuck outta here, fam! The Ones are on the way!" Domino warned. He was standing behind the driver side door of the Chrysler gripping a Desert Eagle.

"Shhhh," The O.G hushed Domino with a finger to his lips, never taking his eyes off of the stud. "I asked you a question, bitch. Speak now, or forever hold your peace." He told her calmly. He was so cool and calm one would have never suspected that he was almost murdered minutes ago.

"Fifty stacks…a hundred if you're alive." She grimaced, tears rolling down her cheeks.

"Who's the nigga that put the dough up?"

She shook her head and said, "I don't know. All we have is a number."

"I'm guessing homie in the beanie has it?" Paybacc inquired, glancing over at the dead man. He figured this because homeboy seemed like he was the leader amongst their pack.

Domino ran through the corpse's pockets until he found a piece of paper with a telephone number scrolled across it. "I got it." He reported to his big homie.

"Well, looks like this is goodbye." Paybacc gave a slight grin and then a scowl. He fired the Tec-9 and it tore off the lower half of the La'chat's face, sending her bloody bottom jaw tumbling down the alley. Her eyes rolled to their whites and her head slammed down on the hood. Her life had expired. "I see homeboy got my message." Paybacc wiped blood from his face and hopped into the Chrysler 300, slamming the door shut behind him. Domino threw the car in reverse and floored it out of the alley backwards. He continued down the street in reverse, spinning around and then gunning away from the murder scene.

It had been one hell of a night.

$$$

Ping!

Clink!

The bloody pellets sounded as Passion pulled them out of Paybacc's arm and shoulder, dropping them into a tin bowl. The O.G sat in a chair backward taking swigs from a bottle of Jack Daniel's to fight the fire in his wounded shoulder and arm. He winced every time Passion fished around inside of the holes in him for the metal slugs with the medical utensil.

Domino sat at the kitchen table with Traquila in his lap while Wacko sat on the arm of the couch throwing back peanuts.

"Damn, kid, fifty thousand?" Wacko inquired, thinking that was a nice piece of change. "Make me wanna put something hot in you and go collect." Paybacc shot him a dirty look before going back to drinking his hard liquor. "I'm fucking with you, cousin. You know you're my nigga if you don't get no bigga."

"Everybody and their momma are going to be looking to collect on that bounty." Domino gave his insight. "We're going to start having to move you around like you're the president or some shit."

"Nah, that will draw too much attention to me. I may as well paint a big target on my chest and write 'put bullets here' on it." Paybacc wiped his mouth with the back of his fist. "Besides, I don't rock with security. I'll leave that to these shook ass niggaz running around out here. All of my life when I had a problem I settled it with this," he held up his fist, "or one of these." He held up the Tec-9 that he used to dust off the stud and the man in the beanie inside of the alley.

"So how do you wanna play it? You wanna go out looking for these niggaz?" Domino caressed Traquila's thick chocolate thigh.

"Ah, shit!" Paybacc hollered in pain, looking to his shoulder.

"That was the last one." Passion told him and dropped the last bloody pellet into the tin bowl. She then went about the task of dressing up his wounds.

Paybacc took the Jack Daniel's bottle to the head. Bringing the bottle down, he licked his lips. "I figure, why go looking for them when we can get 'em to tell us right where they are?"

He smiled devilishly.

Domino and Wacko exchanged confused glances. They had no idea what Paybacc was getting at, but they would soon have clarity.

That was for damn sure.

Chapter Sixteen

Gouch pounded away at a brown tattered punching bag that hung from the ceiling, working up quite the sweat. For the past few weeks Shelly had him going through intense training for the upcoming tournament. The old man had put him on a strict diet, and with exercise he had regained his strength. It was safe to say that Gouch was physically in the best shape of his life.

Gouch stopped working the bag and wiped sweat from his brow with the back of his bandaged wrapped hand. Chest heaving up and down, he sat down on a stool and took a drink of bottle water. From where he sat he watched Shelly gather up the items he needed to shave his head and face. Once he was done gathering everything, he put on a smock and called Gouch over.

"How good are you with a razor?" Shelly asked as he pulled his locks back into a ponytail.

"I've been shaving myself since I was a thirteen." Gouch spoke with confidence.

"Good. Clean me up." Shelly leaned back in the chair and closed his eyes. Gouch got a towel as hot as he could stand it and wrapped Shelly's face with it. He allowed it to stay on him for about five minutes before removing it. After lathering the lower half of his face with shaving cream, Gouch sharpened the straight razor with a strap and brought it below the old man's chin. Adding a little pressure, he brought the straight razor up and left smooth damp skin behind. Next, he placed the razor to Shelly's throat and stopped it there for a moment,

contemplating on whether or not he should cut that mothafucka.

"If I go then we all go," Shelly spoke, startling him. His eyes were still shut. Gouch looked into the dirty, full body mirror and saw his thumb on the button of The Death Trap detonator that could blow everyone to Kingdom Come. "…even my babies." He referred to his dogs. They were all of the family that he had.

Gouch brought the blade up, continuing with his shaving of Shelly. The old man brought the hand that held The Death Trap detonator back under his smock and said, "Good, boy."

He then cleared his throat and allowed Gouch to finish his business.

$$\$\$\$$$

"Heyyyy, I don't clean up so bad for an old man." Shelly smiled as he looked himself over in the full body mirror, turning his head from left to right. He rubbed his stubble face and posed in his reflection. Gouch had shaven off Shelly's locks and gave him a close fade. He also cut off his beard and trimmed it into a thin goatee. The old man's slender frame filled out Gouch's pinstriped suit. His feet were lace in a pair of black Stacy Adams that was polished to a shine. His accessories were a gold necklace with a crucifix and a gold Rolex watch of his own. He'd gotten it when he was caked up. See, although he had almost sold it on many occasions to feed himself and his dogs. He was glad that he hadn't since it complimented his suit so well. "With these new threads and these few dollars I have to throw around, I'm going to fit right in with the rest of those millionaire tycoon types up there." He struck poses in the full body mirror, feeling himself.

Gouch ran a damp warm washcloth from the back of his head and down over his face. He then wringed the towel out into the sink and ran it over his chin and neck. Once he was done, he tossed the washcloth on the sink and felt around his chin and neck. He was baby skin soft and smooth. He was clean shaven. The only hair on his face was the goatee framing his mouth. After putting on a pair of lack cargo pants, he put his foot on the lid of the commode and laced up his combat boots. He stood erect and cracked his knuckles, one fist at a time.

The men's room door vibrated as Shelly knocked on it.

"It's time to roll, young blood." Shelly yelled from behind the door.

Gouch unlocked and opened the door, finding Shelly standing there with a black device that resembled a dog collar. "I got a little gift for you."

He held up the device and smiled.

"What the hell is that?" Gouch frowned, eyes studying the collar.

"The Death Trap is pretty heavy. It'll hold you back when fighting, and the IV in your arm will limit your reach." Shelly informed him on how the machine could limit his capabilities. "We can't very well have you in that contraption, can we? So, I came up with this little doohickey." He locked the collar around Gouch's neck and a green light flashed on. It made one beep and then flashed on neon blue, staying that color. "It's lighter and it'll still get the job done, so don't chu go getting any bright ideas." Shelly mad dogged him. He then unlocked the vest with a key, took it off of his prisoner and hung it up on the wall. Afterwards, he took a camouflage wife beater from out of a bag of clothes and threw it to Gouch. He watched him attentively as he slipped the wife beater on. "All set? Well, let's go. You're driving." He tossed him the car keys.

Shelly put on an overcoat and smacked a black apple-jack on his head, adjusting it at its brim and back. He kissed each one of his dogs on their heads and bid them farewell, waving goodbye as he and Gouch made for the door. Outside, Gouch opened the backseat door of a two tone maroon and silver, Mercedes Maybach Benz. Once Shelly had slid inside, he closed the door and hopped behind the wheel. The vehicle shifted from left to right as Gouch got settled in, buckling his safety belt. Shelly lit up a Black & Mild and polluted the air with smoke. He passed Gouch a piece of paper with the address of the tournament on it. He glanced at the piece of paper then sat it in the ashtray. Once he resurrected the Maybach, he pulled off into the cold night.

$$$

A white limousine drove up a cobble stoned driveway of a mansion. Once it parked, the chauffer hopped out and removed a wheelchair from the trunk. He opened the back door of the limousine and helped Black Jesus into the wheelchair. Once the drug lord was secure in his wheelchair, the chauffer rolled him aside and allowed the rest of his human cargo to emerge. Gangsta stepped into view, followed by Killa Dre. They both were decked out in two piece suits and hard bottom ostrich skin shoes. Killa Dre tugged at the collar of his button-down and loosened his tie. The whole suit thing wasn't really his style, but Gangsta had convinced him to adorn the attire for the occasion. They were going to be mingling with millionaires so he had to dress and conduct himself as one.

"Man, I should have worn a holster; these slacks aren't really keeping this tool up on me." Killa Dre complained as he adjusted the banger on his waistline.

Gangsta looked to the door of the mansion and saw the guests being patted down by the security team as they entered. He turned to his little homie and said, "You're not gonna get in with that heater." He nodded to the door. Killa Dre cursed silently. He whipped the banger from his waistline and laid it at the top of the back tire of their transportation. He then brandished the switchblade from his back pocket, dropped it into his shoe and slid it back on. He would be uncomfortable for a time, but it would be well worth it if something cracked off inside. Gangsta smiled at the young nigga'z improvising and patted him on his back. He draped his arm over his shoulder and they made for the door smiling.

$$$

The mansion's floor was crowded with fighters and their trainers, as well as the millionaires that came out to see the fights. The millionaires sized the fighters up trying to see who they wanted to bet on. They asked the trainers questions and inspected the fighters as if they were race horses. Some fighters stood off in their own space shadow boxing or practicing whatever martial arts they knew. Some prayed to the God of their respective religions, while others kissed their good luck charms or photos of their families. All of them needed or wanted the million dollar prize money; some of them more than others.

"What's up with you? Are you nervous or something?" Shelly asked, seeing the expression on Gouch's face as he paced the floor.

"I don't know," Gouch replied, worry etched across his face. "Could it be the explosive dog collar I'm currently rocking around my neck? I'm not exactly in the mood to jump for joy or tap dance a jig."

"Is that what's got cha panties in a bunch?" Shelly grinned and gripped his shoulder firmly. "I'll tell you what; if you win this tournament for me I'll give you a pardon. How is that?"

"You mean all I gotta do is win this thing, and I'm free to go?" Gouch perked up at the mention of his freedom, cracking the knuckles of both of his fists.

Shelly leaned closer and said, "Hell, I'll even throw in a few bucks."

Gouch looked around at his competition; there were some pretty big and tough looking fighters in the tournament. Some of them really looked like they could put some hands on a nigga in a brawl. He knew taking them on wouldn't be a walk in the park, especially with a million dollars on the line. With that much dough up for grabs, he knew cats were going to be giving this tournament their all, just as he was.

"You've got yourself a deal."

Gouch extended his hand and Shelly gave him a firm handshake.

"Alright then, let's kick these sons of bitches asses then." Shelly smiled, boasting his gray and rotten teeth. They were the only thing that exposed his secret life as a bum. "But keep this in mind, my friend; if you lose then you die." He said seriously, holding up the detonator to his explosive dog collar.

Gouch took a deep breath and silently prayed that the Lord seen him through the challenge.

$$$

Stepping through the door of the mansion, Gangsta was made to place his hand on the screen of the electronic scanner that one of the security guards held out before him. A green laser swept down the screen and a small digital photograph of Gangsta appeared on the display along with his government name: Charles Curtis Vines. There was a chime and *paid* appeared on the screen with two guests beneath it. The security guards then went about the task of giving him and his guests a thorough pat down. Once the pat down was conducted, Gangsta and his guests were free to enter the mansion.

Gangsta, Black Jesus and Killa Dre walked around looking at all of the fighters. They did like the millionaire playboys before them asking questions about the fighters: How long had they been fighting? Who had they fought? What are they trained in? Had they sustained any injuries throughout their career? What's their record? Shit like that.

"See any winners yet?" Gangsta kept his eyes on the fighter when he asked Black Jesus this. At this time he was rolling his good friend around in the wheelchair.

"I have a few in mind." Black Jesus answered as he looked over all of the fighters. There were a few that he thought had the potential to be the champion of the tournament but one particular fighter stood out to him. "Let's check this guy here out." He pointed across the room to an African American fighter. He was one of the few fighters that were shadow boxing, his hands were moving so fast that they looked like blurs to him. An older African American man stood beside him smoking a cigar.

"Jesus Arturo." Black Jesus extended his hand to the trainer.

"Brutus." The trainer shook his hand.

"How long has he been fighting?"

"Old Clayvon's been busting heads and chops for four years now." Brutus gave him the rundown. "Sixty-two fights and zero loses. Guy hasn't met a man he couldn't beat." He boasted proudly as he stuck out his chest. He was a short husky cat with a bushy beard and beady eyes. He wore an apple-jack and a short sleeve shirt that had a stripe on either side, whenever he moved he left the scent of cigar smoke and cheap cologne behind.

"Any injuries?"

"Besides that eye of his, no."

"How'd that happen?"

"That there's a long story."

"Are you his trainer?"

"And friend."

"What is he skilled in?"

"Clayvon's a street fighter; a brawler."

The whole time Black Jesus and the Brutus were conversing, Clayvon was in his zone shadow boxing. His mind had transported him to a place where he was all alone and free to train as he pleased. He was a cat six foot three in height with a muscular physique. He wore his hair in six fuzzy cornrows. An eye-patch lay over his left-eye. A worn brown leather belt held up his green corduroy pants, which lay over his black steel-toe boots.

Forty minutes later

"Gentlemen, may I have your attention, please?" A tall, slender light skinned dude spoke into a microphone. He was dressed in all white. He wore a fedora, shutter shades and a suit under a cape with a red lining. Three gold necklaces lay upon his chest and gold rings decorated all of his fingers on both of his hands. The room settled down and silence swept the audience. Everyone turned around and gave the man their undivided attention. Seeing that he had everyone's attention, white suit continued. "I'd like to thank you all for competing in the tournament tonight. The Ultimate Warrior tournament is the biggest underground fighting tournament there is. We only take in the best of the best. It is here, and only here, that you get to see if you have what it takes against some of the world's finest fighters and have a chance at winning one million dollars in cash." The audience went wild with applause and cheers. Some of the men in the audience whistled when bikini clad beauties came from each side of white suit with clear briefcases of money. The security guards strategically placed around the mansion kept a close eye on the audience and a tight grip on their assault rifles. If anyone was to try to relieve the ladies of their briefcases they were going to get laid down with the quickness. "With that being said, before we get started I'd like all of the fighters to take the time to piss or shit. Or whatever it is you niggaz do before a good fight. The restroom is down the hall and to the left. I'm Kenny Masters, and I'll see you all in fifteen minutes. Peace." He threw up two fingers, swept his cape around and threw something at his feet. There was an explosion of red smoke and when it cleared, white suit and the girls had vanished.

The fighters, trainers and millionaires went about their business. Some went into the restroom, others mingled amongst each other, while the rest took advantage of the food and drinks at the tables against the four walls of the mansion.

"A mill ticket sounds sweet," Killa Dre told Gangsta. "Make a young nigga wanna sign up and try his hand at this shit."

"I know that's right." Gangsta gave him a pound. He casually looked over the room while taking sips from a glass of Cognac over the rocks. Thinking he saw a familiar face, he took a double take. His eyes widen with surprise when they found Gouch practicing for the completion. "Hold this." He passed Killa Dre his glass and made his way towards his oldest nephew, calling his name. Gouch looked to his uncle and was just as surprised to see him. He shook his head no and his kin stopped where he was. Next, he said something to someone in a red pinstriped suit who was trying to mack up on some million dollar pussy. Gouch turned back around to Gangsta, nodded toward the hallway and walked off. Gangsta followed right behind him, getting a good I.D of the old man in the red striped suit as he went along.

$$$

Gouch stretched and bent his limbs and then practiced the martial art he'd been studying since he was a kid: Ninjitsu. He had a ferociousness in his eyes that couldn't be matched by the lion; The King of the Jungle. His fists and legs looked like blurs of mahogany as he threw them up, down and all around. At that moment, if someone were to walk within his space they would be risking getting a broken bone or some flesh seriously bruised. He was throwing his punches, jabs, uppercuts and kicks with that much intensity and force behind them.

Gouch finished his practicing with one last kick high into the air. He held the pose for a time as his chest heaved up and down. He slowly brought his foot back around and placed it to the floor. Hearing someone call his name, he whipped his head around. He was surprised to see that it was Gangsta. Gangsta was making his way through the crowd, but once Gouch gave him a look and shook his head, he stopped in tracks.

"I gotta take a shit, I'll be right back." He told Shelly.

Shelly glanced at his Rolex. "Hurry up. The tournament starts in ten minutes."

Gouch nodded and made his way down the hallway with Gangsta trailing behind him. He ducked off into the rest room and his uncle came in behind him, locking the door. They embraced each other and stepped back.

"Nigga, where the fuck have you been? We've been looking all over for you." Gangsta frowned. Gouch gave him a short summary of what had happen those past few weeks that he was missing. He ended with his being forced into The Ultimate Warrior tournament by Shelly, and if he didn't win then the old man would detonate the explosive dog collar around his neck. Gangsta went to try to remove the dog collar from his neck and he grabbed him about the wrist.

"If you toy with it, then it'll explode." Gouch warned him, eyes bleeding with seriousness.

"Damn. What're we gonna do?"

"I've gotta idea. Listen up."

Chapter Seventeen

The atmosphere reeked of blood and sweat. The white tiled floor had been scrubbed with every cleaning product you could name, buffed and waxed, but there were still faint splotches of blood that wouldn't come up. Many fighters had been left quadriplegics, and some had even lost their lives inside of the savage battle arena. But that didn't stop the two gladiators from going at it like a couple of starving wolves over a fresh kill.

Crack!
Whack!
Thrack!

Clayvon delivered a three punch combination to his opponent that made him stagger back. He'd almost fell but righted himself before his bare back could kiss the floor. After regaining control of his equilibrium, the six-four Russian whipped his head back around. He glared at Clayvon, snapped his broken nose back into place, and wiped the blood from his lip with the back of his bandaged fist. He screamed at the top of his lungs and charged at his opponent.

The millionaires and trainers rooted for the fighter that they wanted to win. There were cheers, hoots and hollers coming from the audience as they were egging their respective fighters on. There were hundreds of thousands of dollars and even some million dollars bets that had been laid. You had to have your dollars up to be able to bet in this fighting league. It was a billion dollar business, and only the wealthiest of the wealthy could throw their hats into the pot.

Clayvon bobbed, weaved and ducked the punches, uppercuts, and hooks that his opponent came at him with. He then came up with an uppercut that was reminiscent of the Mortal Kombat video game. It was so powerful that it split the Russian's jaw in half and sent a mist of blood into the air. The foreigner fell on his back with his eyes rolled to their whites and a crimson mouth. He groaned in excruciation as red streams flowed over his chin. Some of the guys in the audience were pissed while others were in frenzy over the win. The referee, who was a short Puerto Rican man, grasped Clayvon's wrist and raised his hand into the air, declaring him the victor in broken Spanish accent.

"It's because of that kid right there that I'm $500,000 dollars richer." Black Jesus lit up an Arturo Fuentes cigar and took a few puffs. "By the time I leave here I'll have a million dollars."

"Yeah, he and Gouch have been putting in that work," Gangsta stated keeping his eyes on the youngster with the frizzy cornrows. "I'm sitting on two-hundred and fifty kay 'cause of them." He looked across the way to Gouch. He had a towel draped over his head and Shelly was behind him massaging his shoulders. Gouch gave him a slight smirk and winked at him; Gangsta gave him a nod. He then leaned over and whispered into Killa Dre's ear. The young nigga walked backwards until he was swallowed by the audience. One minute later, he emerged on the end of the room where Gouch and Shelly was. He was standing behind Shelly, but he was oblivious to his presence.

The fights went on with body after body crashing onto the floor. Some of the fighters left the arena crippled for life, others left in body bags and the lucky ones left with minor injuries. At the end of the night only two fighters were left to take the floor. Gouch found himself pitted against Clayvon; a man who had ran through his opponents with little difficulty just as he did. Gouch had fought many men in his twenty-seven years on earth, and he'd beaten them all. But somehow he wasn't so sure of himself when it came to his younger opponent. For the first time since he was six years old, and had his first fight, he had butterflies in his stomach.

Gouch bounced from his left leg to his right, bending his neck from left to right. Clayvon's one good eye was dead locked on him; sweat ran over his brow and trickled off of it. He cracked his knuckles but never broke eye contact with his competition.

Kenny Masters stood at the center of both men with a microphone in his hand. He looked between the two fighters, smiling as he brought the microphone to his lips. "Here we are y'all the tournament has been narrowed down to these two fighters. To my right I have, Clayvon 'The Hit-man' Coles," the audience went wild with cheers, "and to my left I have, Gouch 'Crazy Hands' Hood." the audience went wild with cheers again. "This is it my niggaz. The Rumble in the Jungle, The Brawl for it All, the fight that will determine which one of these mothafuckaz will be leaving here with one million dollars in cold, hard cash." He said in a game show host type of voice. He lifted his arm high, and brought it down saying, "Kick ass!"

Ding!
Ding!
Ding!

The bell sounded, lighting fuses in both Gouch and Clayvon. They charged each other, full speed ahead. Nearing one another, they leap into the air and swinging their feet at one another's heads. Their legs connect, duplicating a sound reminiscent of a bamboo stick striking a bamboo tree. The fighters landed to their feet and were quickly back at it, going punch for punch and kick for kick. Clayvon laid into Gouch throwing haymakers for his face and head. Gouch brought his arms up, allowing his arms to absorb the assault. Although none of his opponent's power punches connected, he could feel the bones of his arms throbbing and aching.

Clayvon faked like he was about to throw another haymaker and kicked him on the side of his knee. The searing pain caused Gouch to grimace and drop his guard, leaving his head open for attack. Clayvon swung his steel-toe booted foot around and slammed it into the side of his dome. Seeing himself about to hit the floor, Gouch used his hand to catch himself and brought his feet across Clayvon's face, one foot at a time. The attack made the younger man stumble backwards, but he quickly caught his self. Gouch rushed him again, unleashing a flurry of punches into his torso.

"That's right, get'em!" Shelly egged Gouch on. "Kick his mothafucking ass!"

Crack!

Crack!

Thrack!

Brack!

Gouch stumbled back from the devastating blows, but caught himself, massaging his jaw. Standing erect, he listened to the chants of the audience as they egg him and Clayvon on. The eye-patch rocking fighter walked toward his opponent calmly as if he was strolling through the park.

"Fuck are you doing? Kick his ass!" Shelly barked on Gouch.

"No." Gouch told him.

"What? We had a deal!" Shelly looked at him like he was crazy. He was so close to that million dollars that he could smell it, and here Gouch was about to piss it away.

"Fuck that deal, Blood!"

"You black, bug eyed, burnt face bitch!" Shelly hurled his insults. "I'ma blow your monkey ass up!" Spittle flew from his lips. He was so mad that he couldn't pull the detonator from his pocket fast enough. It snagged on the inside pocket, but he eventually pulled it free. Gouch gave a nod to someone hidden in the audience, just as Shelly was clearing the detonator out of his pocket. The old man's eyes bugged, his nose flared, and his mouth opened as wide as it could as he released a bloodcurdling scream. Killa Dre pulled his switchblade from out of Shelly's calf muscle and wiped it off on his handkerchief.

Seeing the window of opportunity open, Gouch kicked the detonator loose from Shelly's hand. The detonator flew up into the air and he kicked it in Gangsta's direction. Gangsta caught the detonator and smashed it against the handle of Black Jesus' wheelchair until it crumbled into pieces, like a stale cookie.

"No!" Shelly bellowed. He leapt forth and cracked Gouch in the jaw, dropping him. He ran as fast as he could with one good leg toward one of the security guards. The security guard made to shoot him, but his fists were like lighting as they tore into him. He punched him twice in the torso, kneed him and chopped him at the back of his neck. The man howled in pain and crumpled to the floor. Shelly picked up his assault rifle and spun around, spitting rapid fire and laying the other security guards down. The chatter of the weapon caused the audience to scramble and duck for cover, even Kenny Masters was getting the fuck out of dodge. After laying the security guards down, a very pissed off Shelly whipped his weapon around to Gouch. Gouch had just stood to his feet when a single round fled from the barrel of the AK-47. Everything seemed to be moving in slow motion as the missile shaped bullet soared in his direction, rotating counter clockwise.

"Ughhh," Clayvon came out of nowhere tackling Gouch to the floor, narrowly missing the bullet. They hit the linoleum with a thud. Shelly went to fire the AK-47 again and it clicked empty. Seeing Gangsta, Killa Dre, Kenny Masters and Gouch coming after him, the old man tossed the assault rifle aside and made a mad dash toward the door. He threw all of his weight at the locks of the double doors and one of the doors came crashing to the porch. He scrambled to his feet and limped as fast as he could toward his rental. Killa Dre was the first out of the door, followed by Kenny Masters gripping one of the dead security guard's assault rifles.

"Mothafucka, come into my house and fuck my shit up? Unh unh!" Kenny Masters took aim with his assault rifle. Killa Dre came to his side after snatching his gun from off the back tire of the limousine. He pointed his weapon at the fleeing car along with Kenny Masters. They dumped on the car at the same time, shattering its back window and blowing out its back lights. Once they could no longer see the back of the car, they ceased fire and lowered their weapons to their sides. Gouch, Gangsta, Clayvon and Brutus came hurrying down the steps.

"Y'all get'em?" Gouch inquired.

"Naw, mothafucka got away, Blood." Killa Dre said, tucking his tool on his waistline.

"I know where he's going." Gouch informed them.

"Well, let's go. Come on." Gangsta ran back into the mansion to get Black Jesus.

Gouch turned around to Clayvon. "Thanks, man."

"You're welcome." Clayvon shook his hand firmly. "You know you owe me a rematch."

"You got it. If you were pulling those punches I'd hate to see what I'm in store for. But I'll be looking forward to the challenge, though."

The limousine blew its horn.

Gangsta stuck his head out of the back window and waved him on, saying, "Come on, Gucci!"

"Gotta go," Gouch ran off.

Kenny Masters and Clayvon watched the backlights of the limousine until they disappeared into the night. Someone clearing their throat at Kenny's rear gave him cause to turn around.

"Homeboy forfeited, so that million is ours." Brutus said. "I'd like to collect."

Kenny Masters nodded his head and said, "Let me have my guys get rid of these bodies and I'll pay everyone. Come on." He motioned for them to follow him with his assault rifle as he headed for the steps.

$$$

Shelly limped down into the basement as fast as he could, panting out of breath. His dogs rushed to him barking and jumping upon his pants legs, happy to see him. "Not now fellas, daddy's gotta boogie." He grabbed a suitcase that was buried underneath a pile of clothes. He slung it upon the bed and began throwing clothes into it by the handful. He threw a few other things on top of the clothes that he felt was valuable to him. He closed the suitcase, which now had shirt sleeves and pants legs hanging out of it, and grabbed it from out of the bed. He smacked his lucky Dodgers cap upon his head and grabbed his trusty stick. "Come on fellas." He motioned for his dogs to follow him with his stick.

Shelly and his dogs were heading for the door when they heard the basement door being kicked open. The door bounced off of the wall and a stampede of footsteps could be heard hurrying down the steps. Shelly threw down his suitcase and stick. He went to grab the gun from the front of his jeans, but then he realized that he hadn't tucked it. With that in mind, he ran to the place where he stashed his banger, leaving his dogs growling and barking at the doorway.

Shelly had just lifted his mattress and grabbed his Glock when Gouch, Gangsta and Killa Dre came rushing into his doorway. Gouch was lifting his banger to point it at the old man when he was whipping around to take a shot at him. Their fingers curled around the triggers of their weapons at the exact same time.

Bloc!
Boc!

To Be Continued...

Me and My Hittas 4

AVAILABLE NOW BY TRANAY ADAMS

The Devil Wears Timbs 1-7

Bury Me A G 1-5

These Scandalous Streets 1-3

A South Central Love Affair

Me and My Hittas 1-6

The Last Real Nigga Alive 1-3

God Bless the Trappers 1-3

A Gangsta's Empire 1-4

Fangeance

Fear My Gangsta 1-5

A Hood Nigga's Blues

The Realest Killaz 1-3

The Last of the OGs 1-3

The Streets Don't Love Nobody 1-2

The Dopeman's Bodyguard 1-2

King of the Trenches